Peramal

A NOVEL BASED ON A TRUE STORY

Mila Toterah

Though based on a real-life story of the main character, Peramal, some parts of the novel are fictional.

Copyright 2017 Mila Toterah
All rights reserved.

ISBN: 1978248156
ISBN 13: 9781978248151
Library of Congress Control Number: 2017917826
CreateSpace Independent Publishing Platform
North Charleston, South Carolina

For Melinda A.

Peramal (pronunciation: peh-rah-MALL): a noun meaning "clairvoyant," "prophet," "fortune-teller," "oracle."

Chapter 1

Peramal could feel the warm sand trickle down her back as she got up and turned toward the sound coming from behind her. The sun was hot, and it was humid, but it was still another beautiful September day in Clearwater Beach. She shielded her eyes from the sun, forgetting that her sunglasses were on top of her head. The voice was getting louder and louder, and she could barely make out the person coming toward her. Peramal thought maybe she heard her husband's voice, calling out that it was time to get ready to leave for the airport. But this voice sounded very angry and loud, whereas her husband's voice was usually calm and soothing.

"Excuse me, ma'am! Wake up!" The voice grew even louder. "You can't sleep here!"

Peramal was confused; she closed her eyes to clear the blurriness in her vision. She was about argue with the voice when she felt someone pushing against her shoulder.

She opened her eyes and saw that the moon had replaced the sun. It was dark and cold, and the sandy beach was now a hard bench. She looked up to find herself in a park surrounded by tall buildings. Then she remembered that she was in New York—the beautiful beach had just been a dream.

"Ma'am, get your kids and go to a shelter, or I will have to arrest you for loitering and your kids will end up in foster care," Officer Denali threatened. Then his voice softened a bit and he said, "Do you really want me to have to do that?" Denali knew that bad things can happen to kids in foster care. Everyone has a story, but he didn't know hers, and he tried not to make any assumptions. He actually felt sorry for her.

Peramal immediately noticed how blue his eyes were—so blue that she got lost in them. Even in the dark, they stood out so brilliantly. She didn't realize that he had stopped talking and was waiting for her to answer. She finally responded.

"I'm sorry, officer, but all of the shelters were full. We didn't have any place to go."

"Well, I better not find you when I come back around again," he said as he started to walk away. He didn't want his partner to catch up with him and find her there; Officer Verde wouldn't be so forgiving.

"Thank you, Officer," Peramal said, relieved that he had let them go. Then, a thought crossed her mind, and she was compelled to speak to the officer once more.

"Excuse me, Officer, but do you play the lottery?" she asked. "If you don't, you should. I know you don't believe me and probably think I am crazy. Guess I can't blame you. Thanks again for letting us go." She said all that in one breath.

Officer Denali turned back around to face her, looking confused. She was right; he *had been* thinking that she was out of her mind. He couldn't figure her out, and he wasn't sure how to respond. All he kept on thinking was how beautiful she was, but, still, he wanted her to leave before Verde showed up. "You're welcome" was all he could muster before he turned away.

Peramal waved at him. Then she looked down to find her eleven-year-old son and five-year-old daughter still asleep on the park bench. It broke her heart that this was happening to them and her.

"Mis amores, we need to get up and go," she whispered. The young children started rousing from their sleep.

"Mama, I am hungry and cold," her daughter, Melinda, said, rubbing her eyes to wake up. Her son, Victor, stood up without a word and started to gather their blankets and the black trash bags used to carry what little they had. He was her rock and never complained. Victor was tall and strong for his age, so that he was able pick up Melinda. He cradled her in his arms—she was quite the tiny thing—and they started to walk away.

"Where are we going?" Melinda said. Her voice, which quivered slightly, sounded muffled from being against Victor's chest.

"We are going to try and find Cousin Alberto, and we will get food and get warm," her mother tried to console her.

Peramal had lied to the officer about the shelter. They had found a place in one, but it took only five minutes before she was being propositioned for sex in order to be able to stay there. When she tried to complain, they just laughed at her.

She gathered her children and their belongings and left. It was too dark to be able to find their way around the city, so they had found a park bench in Central Park—where the police then found them.

As they walked along the dirty sidewalk, Peramal could see the sun starting to rise in the distance. *Another day in paradise*, she thought to herself sarcastically.

Her thoughts then drifted back to the dream. Oh, how she loved that dream; this time, though, it had felt more real than usual. But she knew that it would never come true. For her, only the bad dreams did, never the good ones.

Peramal had been born with a gift of seeing the future—at first, in a glass of water; other times, through thoughts flashing in her mind; and sometimes in her dreams. Her earliest memory of being "special" was from when she was four years old. She knew things before she ever heard them. It scared her sometimes, but it also got her in a lot of trouble. She would blurt things that came to her mind, and people would accuse her of eavesdropping. It especially angered her mother, who would send Peramal to her room without dinner—more times than she could count. Sometimes she tried to stay away from people, to block thoughts out of her head. But over time she learned to control it.

Her given name was Perla Maria, but her father nicknamed her Peramal, which means "fortune-teller." Her papa was very proud of her and didn't treat her like an outcast, like the rest of her family had. But all that had changed on her eighth birthday, in June 1979. They found his body on a rainy afternoon along a roadside in San Juan; the police never figured out what had happened to him, and no one was brought to justice. Peramal knew that bad people had killed him while looking for money.

As if he was reading her thoughts, Victor's voice startled her. "Mama? How come you won't read the water for people so that you can make money?" he asked. "A. J. said that you are a witch and that you could make a lot of money! If we had the money, A. J. wouldn't have kicked us out of his house!" He lowered his sister to her feet because his arms were getting tired and he wanted to rest them. Melinda fell in step between her brother and her mother, holding each of their hands.

"A. J. does not know what he is talking about, and don't ever call me a witch again!" Peramal said angrily. "It's not that simple. It's not right to take money for such a thing. I will do it to help people, but sometimes it gets to be too much for me. Maybe when you are older, you will understand it," she said, as she prayed that her son would stop with the questions. "Now, let's see what we're going to do."

Her son stared up at her with tears in his eyes. "I'm sorry, Mama."

Peramal felt bad that she had yelled at him. She held him close and assured him that everything would be OK as they started walking down the sidewalk in the cold morning.

❈

The smell of coffee and baked goods filled the air as the city was waking up.

Denali was heading to meet up with his partner at the diner for their usual breakfast at the end of their shift before they went home. They had been on patrol all night in the Central Park area because of the recent rash of muggings.

On the way to the diner, he couldn't stop thinking about that young woman in the park. *What could have happened to her that she ended up this way?* he thought to himself, but then he tried to put her out of his mind.

That only worked for all of five minutes. When he passed by the all-night liquor store next to the diner, he remembered what she had said about playing the lottery. He thought he would give it a try, so he bought a scratch-off—what did he have to lose except a couple of bucks? To his surprise, he won a hundred dollars!

He couldn't believe it; she had been right. So he bought another scratch-off, but he didn't win anything the second time. "I guess I can't get too greedy," he mumbled to himself.

He collected his winnings and went to the diner to meet up with his partner.

Verde was sitting at a booth next to the window drinking coffee when he noticed Denali coming out of the liquor store before entering the diner.

"Hey, Eddie, isn't it too early to be drinking before breakfast?" he asked him in a very deep New York accent. Verde's voice resonated throughout the diner as Edward lowered himself into the booth.

"She's finally done it! Your wife has driven you to drink! I always told you Cecelia was high maintenance!" Verde teased him. Paul Verde liked to kid around a lot when he wasn't working—but it was hard to tell that he was joking because of the constant scowl on his face. They had been working together since Edward had joined the force ten years ago. They trusted each other with their lives because they had seen it all together.

"Would you keep it down, Verde!" Edward said in a hushed voice. "Half the block probably heard you!"

Before Verde got the chance to ask more questions, the waitress came over to take their orders, and Verde forgot all about his visit to the liquor store. Denali was relieved; he wasn't sure how he could explain about the woman in the park and the lottery win.

They polished off a breakfast of scrambled eggs, toast, bacon, and a side of pancakes. As they were finishing the last of their coffee, it started to rain hard, with thunder and lightning.

Edward looked outside across the street and noticed a woman with two children, all of them running down the sidewalk carrying trash bags.

They look familiar, he thought to himself. Then he realized *it was them!*

"Ah, great! There goes my golf game!" Verde lamented, with Denali only half listening to him. He was too busy trying to find out where they were going.

Edward turned his head toward his partner when he saw him get up and leave.

"All right, Eddie, I will see you later. Thanks for breakfast!" Verde smiled as he walked away without waiting for a response.

At that point, Edward didn't care that was he stuck with the check again; he turned his attention back to the mystery woman and her kids outside. But they were gone. It's was like they'd vanished into thin air. He quickly put cash on the table and ran outside.

Chapter 2

Peramal and her children walked the streets of New York City for several hours as she tried to figure out what to do next—and then it started to rain. She hated the rain; it reminded her of the day that had changed her life forever.

They found themselves in front of an abandoned warehouse.

"Here. Let's go in here. We will be safe for now." Peramal tried the door handle, but it was locked. She instinctively knew that there was a key hidden somewhere. She felt around door's edge and found one. They walked in to find the space empty except for a couple of chairs and a table, an inch-thick layer of dust, and couple of unwanted visitors scurrying around. It was cold and drafty, but at least they were inside and out of the rain.

Peramal picked up the table and chairs and wiped off the dust. She picked up one the trash bags, into which she'd snuck food before her brother kicked them out: a loaf of bread, a jar of peanut butter, a bottle of water, and an apple. They each took turns biting into the apple, and had a small piece of bread and a sip of water. They finished eating the small amount of food allotted so that they could ration the food for as long as they could.

"Let's get the blankets so you can try and get some rest," Peramal told her children. "There's too much lightning. Victor, I need you to stay here with your sister. I'll go and find a pay phone to call Cousin Alberto."

Victor nodded.

"No, Mama! Please don't go! I'm scared!" Melinda cried.

"It's OK, my love; your brother will take care of you, and I'll be back soon. OK? Don't forget to lock this door!"

Without waiting for a response, the young mother kissed her daughter and son and left.

Melinda and Victor felt scared and alone. The young girl clutched the doll that she was carrying as she stood staring at the door her mother had left through. She started to cry, with the tears falling silently down her cheeks.

"Victor, do you think Mama is coming back for us?" Melinda asked quietly.

"Of course she is! Why would you ask that question!" Victor responded in a frustrated tone. "Now, come here and sit down so that no one will see you through the window."

The little girl listened to her brother and sat next to him on the floor; they both had their backs propped up against the wall.

"Victor?" Melinda once again was full of questions. "Are we ever going back home?"

"I don't know!" he responded angrily. "Enough with the questions!"

Peramal

A loud sound at the door startled the children. Someone was trying to push his or her way in.

"Mama! Mama!" Melinda screamed and ran to the door to open it before Victor had the chance to stop her.

"Melinda! No! Don't open the door!" he said, yelling at her. But it was too late. The door swung open, and a police officer was standing there, getting drenched in the rain.

❖

Peramal wanted to go out and find help, but not from Cousin Alberto, as she had led her children to believe. She couldn't figure how the children even knew Cousin Alberto's name—then she remembered: they must have overheard her brother say that name when they were arguing before A. J. threw them out. In actuality, Alberto was the last person that she wanted to see. She had been twelve years old when Alberto got drunk at a party one night at her grandmother's house in Puerto Rico and then raped her. Alberto had made it sound like Peramal had come onto him, and she was blamed for it. Her grandmother didn't believe her and called her a whore.

Her thoughts were interrupted when she noticed that she was walking by a church. She crossed the street and went inside. It was beautiful, and she felt safe. Peramal sat in a pew and then kneeled. Lost in prayer, Peramal didn't realize someone had come in and sat next to her, on the opposite side of the aisle.

"Hello." The elderly gentlemen spoke first.

"Good morning," Peramal responded and then turned back to her prayer.

"You look lost," said the stranger.

"I am OK. Thank you."

"You need to go back."

She turned back around to ask what he meant and found that he had disappeared. She looked around and didn't find him, and then it hit her: "Melinda! Victor!"

She took off like a bolt of lightning, running as fast as she could back to the warehouse. There was a police car parked in front, with Melinda and Victor sitting in the back. The officer started to drive away; he didn't see Peramal screaming while she ran behind the car.

Chapter 3

"Rain, rain, go away, come again another day!" The young girl sat by the window, humming the song to herself as she watched the rain. Peramal had wanted to go outside, but it was raining hard, and it was very windy. It was the beginning of June—the rainy season in Puerto Rico. She was waiting for her father to come home, but it was getting late, and her mother was getting very worried.

Iris, Peramal's mother, was an American from New York, while her father, Antonio, was from Puerto Rico. They had met when her father—a traveling salesman—was on a business trip in New York City.

They had gotten married, much to the dismay of Antonio's mother, and Iris had moved with him to Ponce, a small city in Puerto Rico about a two-hour drive from the capital, San Juan. In the beginning, they were happy, but as time went on, the isolation started to wear on Iris and their marriage. Antonio had thought that after they had the kids, things would get better for Iris. But the resentment grew, especially Iris's resentment toward the kids. Times were getting tough, and Antonio was spending a lot of time away from home trying to earn a living.

Peramal had an older brother, Antonio Jr., but people called him A. J. for short. Peramal was born two years after A. J., and three years after that, they had a sister, Sophia. Iris never learned to speak Spanish, and she wouldn't allow her kids to either—at least, they couldn't do so in the house. They had to know it for school. But Peramal loved the Spanish language and would secretly talk with her father whenever he was in town.

It was almost Peramal's birthday; she was turning eight. She was excited about her birthday, but she knew something was wrong. She kept seeing her father appear in the corner of her eye, but when she turned to look, he would disappear. He had gone on a business trip a week ago and was supposed to be home already. Peramal had terrible dreams the whole time he was gone; she would wake up screaming in the middle of the night, looking for him. Instead of consoling her, her mother would yell at her to shut up and would threaten to send her to her grandmother's (Antonio's mother's place). Sometimes Iris would come in the room and slap Peramal if she didn't stop the crying, because it was disturbing Iris's sleep.

The sound of the rain was drowned out by her mother's screaming. "Who was in my room trying on my makeup!" she yelled angrily. "Peramal! I know it was you!" she yelled as she stomped her way to the living room to confront her daughter.

"Mama! It wasn't me; it was Sophia!" Peramal cried as her mother started to smack her. Sophia stood at the doorway with a smile on her face. She was always trying to get Peramal in trouble. Sophia knew that Peramal was her papa's favorite, and she did everything she could to be her mother's favorite in return. In their mother's eyes, Sophia could do no wrong, even though she was the one that had a smudge of lipstick on her face.

Just then, there was a loud knock on the door.

"Are you Iris Otero, and is your husband, Antonio Roberto Otero?" Officer López asked while his partner, Officer Martínez, showed her the driver's license.

"Yes, I am. Is something wrong?" Iris cried.

"I regret to inform you that your husband was found deceased along the side of the road. I need you to come with me to identify the body," Officer López spoke in a matter-of-fact voice. He hated delivering this type of news. There was always drama, and sometimes it was hard for him to get in a word edgewise. He didn't mean to sound so cold, but if he let himself care about every situation, he would be too depressed to come to work.

Iris screamed in anger and turned her attention to Peramal. "It is your fault! You did this to him! You had your dreams, and it came true! I always knew you were a witch! I hate you!"

"I'm sorry, Mama! I didn't mean to! I'm sorry! I'm sorry!" Peramal repeated as she cried in anguish.

The officers felt sorry for the little girl. "Please, Mrs. Otero, calm down. This was not your daughter's fault." Officer Martínez spoke up first.

Iris was angry and was about to lash out at the officers, but common sense finally took over when she realized what she was doing and she noticed each of the officers had his hand on his gun holster.

"I'm sorry. I will go get ready," her mother said as she closed the door and turned to give Peramal a cold stare. "A. J., stay here with your sisters."

Peramal ran to the window to look outside and saw the officers standing on the porch. She waved at them and smiled as her way to thank them for coming to her defense. Both officers smiled back and waved.

The next few weeks were filled with tears and anger. After the funeral, Iris found out that her husband was thousands of dollars in debt and there was no money in the bank account. Their home was taken over by debt collectors. Peramal and her family were homeless and penniless. They had to move in with her grandmother.

Peramal's grandmother's house was small and did not have enough beds, so Peramal had to sleep on the floor. After all, according to her mother, it was Peramal's fault that they were in this mess in the first place. In fact, everyone in the family blamed Peramal for her father's death, and she did not understand why. She couldn't help these dreams that came true, and she didn't know how or why sometimes she could predict the future.

Peramal was made responsible for all of the cooking and cleaning. She was only allowed to leave the house to go to school, which was a treat for her.

At the house, Sophia and A. J. did not have to lift a finger to do anything. Sophia got to sleep in a nice room with her mother, and A. J. got the attic (which had a bed in it), while

Peramal

Peramal had to sleep on the floor. Some nights, she would be lucky to sleep on the sofa when her father's sister, Letti, and Letti's husband, Luis, weren't visiting.

Sometimes Luis would come lie down next to Peramal where she was sleeping on the floor. While touching her breasts, he would put his fingers in her vagina.

"You are a special little girl. You are so beautiful," Luis would say. "I want us to be friends, and I could take care of you and you take care of me. I will teach you," he whispered in her ear, with his breath reeking of alcohol.

Peramal knew that this was wrong, but she would stay quiet and pretended to be asleep. One night, Luis was more drunk than usual and didn't stop at just touching her. She fought back, but he was too strong for her. She knew that if she said anything about it, they would blame her and kick her out of the house.

She knew someday soon he wasn't coming back ever. The very next day, Luis died in a car accident. Peramal's aunt did survive, but she broke her pelvis and was bed-bound for weeks. Letti moved in, and Peramal couldn't go to school anymore, because her aunt needed someone there all the time to wait on her hand and foot.

It was six months and one day after her father died that she came home from the market to find that her mother had taken her sister and brother and gone back to New York without Peramal.

"Abuela? Where are Mama, Sophia, and A. J.?" Peramal asked her grandmother, who was sitting at the kitchen table, nursing a cup of tea. She already knew the answer but was hoping she was wrong.

"She left," her grandmother responded in Spanish, in a monotone voice.

"But where did she go? Is she coming back for me?" Peramal asked, on the verge of tears.

"I don't know where she went, and she is not coming back for you," replied Peramal's grandmother. Then she got up and walked away.

Peramal stood in the middle of the kitchen feeling a wave of emotions, especially abandonment and fear. *Tick, tick, tick*—she could hear the clock from the living room as she stood motionless in the middle of the kitchen.

"Perla Maria! Perla Maria!" the sound of aunt's voice boomed in the quiet kitchen. "I'm hungry! Get me something to eat!"

Peramal held back tears as she went to the refrigerator to make lunch for her aunt. She willed herself to feel nothing, absolutely nothing.

Chapter 4

Aunt Letti finally moved out of Peramal's grandmother's house almost a year after the accident. She had met another man, and they started living together. Letti's boyfriend had a son who moved in as well. Peramal knew that her aunt's boyfriend was only using her, and she tried to warn her that he was going to steal the money that Letti had received as a result of a lawsuit following the car accident. But Letti just laughed at her and accused her of being jealous.

Peramal tried to resume a normal life as much as she could; she went back to school. But school was tough. She was constantly picked on and harassed because everyone knew that she was an orphan—that her father had died, and her mother didn't want her.

"Oh, look at the little crybaby, boohoo! Nobody wants me!" An eighth-grade girl named Juana taunted her. She would yell at Peramal across the school yard, and everyone would laugh.

It didn't help that Peramal had developed early and was constantly getting unwanted attention from the boys. Many times she was accused of stealing other girls' boyfriends.

Peramal did everything she could to cover herself with oversized shirts, but that didn't work. Most school days, she spent recess and lunch in the library. She escaped to the world of books, and the books were her friends.

One night in April, her grandmother had a get-together, and basically everyone got drunk. Her father's cousin, Alberto, raped her while in a drunken stupor. The music was loud, and no one could hear her screaming. After that night, she vowed that it would never happen again. Peramal started sleeping with a knife under her pillow.

The dreams started coming again on her twelfth birthday. But this time it was different. She saw herself sitting at the kitchen table with her grandmother, looking in a glass of water, and she knew about things in the future. In the water she saw that her grandmother was sick and was going to die in a terrible way. Peramal woke up in a cold sweat. She got up and ran to her grandmother's room to make sure she was all right. Her grandmother was sleeping soundly.

The next morning, Peramal woke up to find her grandmother sitting at the kitchen table with a clear glass filled with water in front of her, like Peramal had seen in her dream. She motioned for her granddaughter to sit down.

"Come. Read for me," her grandmother said in Spanish.

"But, I don't understand," replied Peramal with fear in her voice.

"Your gift. This is how you can use it. Let's see if it is strong enough," Abuela responded. "You are old enough now."

Peramal

Peramal sat down. Her hands were shaking as she grabbed the cup, spilling some of the water.

"¡Estúpida! Be careful what you are doing!" her grandmother reprimanded her. "Now, I am going to put my hand over the cup, and you will put yours on top of mine and concentrate."

"OK, but why me?" Peramal asked. "How did I get this?"

"My mother had the gift, and I thought I did too. But I didn't. When you dreamed about your papa and it came true, I knew you truly had it," Abuela explained with resentment in her voice. "Now you need to learn how to use it so that you can earn your keep and make money."

"But...but...why didn't you tell my mama that I wasn't a witch that it was not my fault papa died!" Peramal's voice quivered as she started to cry.

Abuela slapped Peramal across the face. "Don't you talk back to me, you ungrateful brat!" she yelled at her granddaughter. "I did you a favor! I knew you mother would leave after your father died, God rest his soul." She made the sign of the cross. "I wasn't about to let that *americana* take you away. I knew I could make a lot of money off you."

Peramal just sat there in stunned silence, with her hand on her cheek where her grandmother had slapped her. She knew that, somehow, she had to find her mother and explain everything. She knew that someday she had to get to New York.

"Oh, now you are crying! Forget it, it's not going to work today. You better be ready tomorrow or I will kick you out to the street! You hear me!" Abuela said, with controlled anger in her voice. She got up and walked away.

Peramal ran to her room, locked the door, and cried herself to sleep. But it was a restless sleep. She kept seeing her mother; she was standing on a beach, and the sun was shining, and everything was beautiful. Both Sophia and A. J. were with her, and they were talking and laughing. *Here is my chance*, she thought to herself. She called out to get their attention, but they never would turn around. Then she tried to run to her mom, but she couldn't move. She tried to scream, but no sound came out.

"Mama, it was not my fault that Papa died! I have this gift, and it tells me things! Please come to me! It's not my fault! It's not my fault!" She woke up drenched in sweat, with her face full of tears as she repeated the phrase. Then she realized that she was still in Puerto Rico and she has no idea where to start to find her mother.

The next day, she sat once more with her grandmother and read the water. She told her grandmother about things from the past and present. Her grandmother wasn't satisfied; she wanted the future.

"Concentrate!" her grandmother yelled at her. What Peramal didn't tell her was that her grandmother didn't have much of a future. She saw her grandmother die, but she was afraid to say anything. Sometimes she thought about lying to her grandmother, but she knew that would be wrong.

Mrs. Gonzálezs, her grandmother's neighbor, stopped by one day for coffee, but her grandmother was upstairs taking a nap.

Peramal

"*¡Hola!* Mrs. González, how are you?" Peramal greeted the older woman. She liked Mrs. González, who was always kind to her.

"*¡Hola*, Peramal! Nice to you see you! Oh my, you are growing up to be a beautiful young lady!" Mrs. González said kindly. Peramal smiled.

"Abuela is taking a nap. Would you like to sit down and I can make you some coffee?" Peramal offered.

"*Sí, sí*, that would be nice." Mrs. González sat at the table while Peramal was making the coffee.

When she had finished making the coffee, Peramal sat down across from Mrs. González.

"Your grandmother tells me you can read the water. Is that true?" Mrs. González asked.

"Well, I am not sure if I am any good at it," Peramal replied.

"Would you try for me? I am sorry to ask you, but I am worried about my daughter. She has been married two years and still hasn't gotten pregnant," Mrs. González said. "I am afraid her husband is going leave her."

Peramal felt sorry for her and wanted to help.

She stood up, got a clear glass from the cabinet, and poured water in it.

Then she put it on the table and had Mrs. González put her hand on it. She covered the glass with her own hand and prayed. Then she picked up the glass of water and was shocked to see different things pop out.

"I think you are going to hear about a baby very soon. I hope it is for your daughter, but I know it is someone in the family,"

Peramal said to Mrs. González. "But, you have to believe it and be positive and pray. I will pray for her too!

"And don't worry about your daughter's husband; he is a good man and loves your daughter very much," Peramal continued.

"Thank you, God!" Mrs. González clutched her hands in prayer. "From your lips to God's ear!"

"Don't worry, you will come and tell me the good news," Peramal smiled as she assured the older lady.

Mrs. González grabbed her purse and opened it to give Peramal money. "Please take this!" Mrs. González implored.

"No! No! I don't want your money; I only wanted to help you. I didn't do anything." Peramal pushed the money back into Mrs. González's hand.

Just then, Abuela walked into the kitchen.

"Oh, Mrs. González, how nice to see you," Abuela said.

"Hola, Mrs. Otero, your granddaughter was kind enough to read for me, and I tried to pay her, but she didn't want to take it," Mrs. González explained.

Abuela gave Peramal a cold stare and reached out to take the money.

"Thank you, Mrs. González. I hope you were happy with the reading," Abuela said.

"Yes, I feel better, and I hope Peramal is right!" Mrs. González responded as she said her good-byes and left.

Peramal was feeling happy that she had done something good and helped someone. As she was clearing the coffee cups from the table, Abuela smacked her upside the head so hard that she fell to the floor.

"Don't you ever turn down money! You hear me!" Abuela yelled at her. Peramal had never seen her look so angry.

About a week had gone by when Mrs. Gonzáles came knocking on the door. Peramal answered the door, and Mrs. Gonzáles came in and hugged the young girl. The older lady was excited and practically in tears.

"You were right, Peramal! My daughter just found out she is pregnant! Thank you, thank you!" Mrs. González spoke happily.

Word got around fast about what Peramal had predicted for Mrs. González's daughter, and everyone wanted to talk to her. Her grandmother's plan had worked.

Peramal was reading for at least a dozen people every week, and she was so exhausted that it was making her physically ill. She was absorbing all of the bad energy, and it was wearing her down. She tried to tell her grandmother, but she wouldn't listen. Abuela was enjoying the extra income from the readings too much. Peramal did not get any of the money, and that was how she wanted to keep it. Peramal knew that it was wrong to gain financially from her God-given gift. She prayed every night, asking for forgiveness.

Sometimes people didn't like what they heard and wanted their money back. No one understood that she did not control what she saw and that sometimes it was better to let things work themselves out as they should. But that advice always fell on deaf ears.

This went on for the next three years. She was about to turn fifteen when her grandmother and aunt took pity on her and decided that maybe they should have a birthday party for her *quinceañera*. This would be the first time in years that she had celebrated her birthday.

She didn't have a dress to wear for her birthday, and her grandmother wouldn't buy her one. Abuela told Peramal to make do with what she had—which was nothing.

On a hot and humid day, three days before her birthday party, Peramal decided to go for a walk in town. Even though she couldn't buy anything, she could dream.

As Peramal passed by Mrs. González's house, she saw the older lady outside with her two-year-old grandson.

"*¿Cómo está, Señora González?*" Peramal said, smiling and waving as she passed by.

"*¡Hola, Peramal!* How nice to see you!" Mrs. González said excitedly. "Here is my grandson!"

"He is beautiful! God bless him!" Peramal stopped to see the baby.

"Guess what! My daughter is pregnant again! Thank you for your reading and prayers! You blessed my life!" Mrs. González said as she hugged Peramal with one arm while holding her grandson with the other.

"I think it might be a girl this time," Peramal said with a smile.

"*Sí, sí!* you are right! God bless you, my child! Are you ready for your birthday party? Did you get a dress? I bet you will look beautiful!" Mrs. González said all in one breath.

Peramal looked embarrassed. "No, I can't afford it. But that is OK. No problem. I don't need it."

"Well! We can't have that! Come into my house! I bet I will have one of my daughter's dresses that you can borrow," Mrs. González said excitedly.

Peramal thanked Mrs. González and said it was not necessary, but she insisted. It was no use arguing with her.

Mrs. González's daughter had several beautiful dresses: some long, and some short. She had never seen so much lace and chiffon. Peramal picked a simple, green-chiffon dress that looked beautiful when she tried it on. It brought out the green color of her hazel eyes.

Once again, Peramal thanked the older lady and went home, happily carrying the dress.

When the day came, Peramal got dressed for her party. She applied very little makeup because she didn't really need it. Her light-olive complexion was flawless, and her eyes were wide, captivating, and mysterious—almost cat-like, with long, dark eyelashes. Her hair was light brown with natural highlights and curls. After piling her hair on top of her head with some of its soft ringlets falling around her face, she made her way down the stairs.

The music was playing loudly, and several people were standing, around including her aunt's boyfriend and his eighteen-year-old son, named Julio.

Julio was getting bored and didn't think that it was much of a party. His father, Juan, had convinced him to stay to meet the birthday girl.

"No! No! Don't go! You have to meet Peramal. She is a real looker!" Juan said. "Don't worry, she does not look anything like her aunt." And for once, Julio's father was right. Julio noticed her as soon as she walked in the room.

Peramal felt someone staring at her. She quickly saw who it was. He was so handsome and tall. He was smoking a cigarette and drinking a beer. Her heart started to race when she saw him coming toward her. His hair was jet-black, and his eyes were dark brown.

"Hi. You must be Peramal. I'm Julio Collazo." He spoke close to her ear so that she could hear him over the music. She smelled the cigarettes and alcohol on his breath and felt a shiver as he whispered in her ear.

All she could say was "hello." She was speechless, which was unusual since she always had something to say and spoke her mind.

"You are so beautiful." He continued to speak in a soft tone, directly into her ear. "Your auntie didn't tell me this, or else I would have wanted to meet you a long time ago."

She blushed with embarrassment and stuttered a "thank you." Then Julio took her by the hand and said, "Let's go somewhere less noisy."

This was the first time Peramal ever remembered feeling special and beautiful. She had always dreamed of her Prince Charming coming to rescue her. But the man of her dreams who stood before her now would eventually became her worst nightmare.

Chapter 5

Julio and Peramal became inseparable after her birthday party. Her grandmother was not pleased about their relationship because she did not want Peramal to lose her focus. But Julio worked his charm, and her grandmother gave in. In fact, she allowed him to move in. Peramal felt that things were finally going her way. But that feeling didn't last long.

Three months later, Julio's father drained the money from Aunt Letti's bank account and took off without a word, just as Peramal had warned her. Once again, Letti moved back in with Peramal's grandmother. However, this arrangement made things very difficult, since Julio was a constant reminder of how Letti had lost her money. Letti was constantly arguing with Julio, asking him where his father had gone.

Meanwhile, Julio lost his job and started hanging around the house all the time, constantly arguing with Letti. Julio was getting on everyone's nerves, except for Peramal's. He was her knight in shining armor. Letti wanted Abuela to throw Julio out, but Abuela knew that Peramal would leave along with him, and she did not want to lose her extra source of income. As long as Peramal did her readings, she served a purpose.

One night, Julio and Peramal were in the living room, watching TV. Her aunt and grandmother were at Don Carlo's, gambling away the money that Peramal had earned that day.

Out of the blue, Julio asked Peramal to marry him. But, he told her to keep it a secret. She was so excited, she agreed to whatever he asked. It had always been her dream to wear a beautiful white dress. Julio also told her that he was looking for a job and that it would be a while before they could get married, with the white dress and everything. So instead he suggested that they elope.

"How about we go and get married at the courthouse?" Julio asked Peramal. "That way, you and I can be together forever, starting now."

Peramal didn't know what to say. She wanted to say "yes," but she was afraid that her grandmother would get angry.

"Julio, there is nothing I'd rather do than marry you. But Abuela is not going to be happy. She will say that we are too young," she explained to Julio.

"But you love me, don't you? Or maybe you don't?" he said in a threatening voice.

"Yes! Of course I do!" she cried, afraid that she might lose him.

"Then are you going to do it?" he asked again.

"OK," she whispered. She knew that she didn't have a choice if she didn't want to lose him.

So the next morning, they went to downtown and got married without telling anyone.

Peramal

About a week later, Abuela was sitting at the table counting the money from the readings. It had been a really busy week. With the threat of a hurricane looming, people were scared and wanted to know if they would be OK.

Julio walked in, and Peramal's grandmother quickly put the money away.

"That is a lot of money, Abuela. Don't you think that Peramal should get half of it, or maybe all of it?" Julio said in a threatening tone. "She is the one that does the work!"

"It is none of your business! This is between me and my granddaughter!" she replied angrily.

"I don't think so, old lady! It becomes my business when it involves my wife!" Julio yelled back.

"No! You liar!" Peramal's grandmother screamed at him. "How could she do this to me!"

At that point, Peramal walked in the kitchen door from outside.

"Is it true, Peramal? Did you marry him?" Peramal's grandmother attacked her as soon as she walked in the door.

Peramal was afraid. Putting her head down, she whispered, "Yes."

Abuela lunged at her, but Julio got in between them and pushed the older lady back, onto a chair.

"You whore! How dare you get married behind my back!" she yelled at her granddaughter. "I will deal with you later! Julio, get out of my house!"

Without a word, Julio grabbed the envelope of money and his wife's hand and ran out of the house, vowing to never return.

Peramal could hear her grandmother yelling and cursing behind them. As she and Julio ran out of the house, Peramal knew that she was never going to see her grandmother again.

Abuela was angry and upset, and couldn't believe that Julio had taken the money. She knew he was trouble, just like his father. Deep in her heart, she knew what she had done to Peramal was wrong, but she couldn't stop herself. She needed that money; she was heavy in debt with Don Carlo. The ringing phone interrupted her thoughts. Abuela was afraid that it was Don Carlo looking for his money for the week. But instead it was Iris, Peramal's mother.

"I sent the check already!" she yelled at Iris. "But there isn't going to be any more! Your daughter ran off with a boy! So stop calling me!" she slammed the phone. She wasn't about send any more money to that *americana*; she needed it all for herself. Luckily, she had saved enough to pay Don Carlo a weekly, agreed-upon amount until she figured out a new plan. Right now, she needed a nap, so she went to bed.

Chapter 6

It had been six months since that day in the kitchen at Peramal's grandmother's house. Peramal and Julio had gone to Julio's old neighborhood in San Juan, which was a two-hour bus ride away.

Ms. Mari, a seamstress at a local dress shop, was making herself some dinner that night. It had been a long day at work. It was hard to tell that Ms. Mari was in her early fifties because of her youthful features. Her black her was long and straight, but she often wore it wound up in a bun. She was average height, with a slender build.

Just as she was about to sit down and eat, a knock at the door startled her. It was her nephew, Julio, who had a beautiful young girl with him.

Julio was her sister's son. She had promised her younger sister on her deathbed that she would always watch out for Julio, which was very difficult—especially at times when he would fall into the wrong crowd and didn't care about who he was hurting along the way. The fact that Julio's father had left him after stealing money didn't help.

But tonight was different, and she knew that girl with Julio was someone special. Ms. Mari didn't ask any questions. She took pity on them and let them stay at her house until Julio could find a job and they could go and rent a place of their own.

Peramal helped around the house and did the cooking and cleaning. Peramal really liked Julio's aunt; Ms. Mari was kind to her and treated her like her own daughter. Ms. Mari had been married, but they didn't have any children. When she turned forty, her husband had decided to leave her for someone half her age.

One evening, Ms. Mari came home with a dress that she needed to finish by the next day. Her arthritis was acting up, and it was difficult for her to manipulate the needle.

"*Buenas noches*, Ms. Mari," Peramal greeted her with a smile. "Do you want something to eat?"

"Hola, Peramal," Ms. Mari answered. "No, I am not hungry, *gracias*. Just tired. But I have to get this done."

She showed Peramal a white wedding dress. It was missing at least fifty tiny buttons.

"I can help you, if you like," Peramal offered.

"Do you know how to sew?" Ms. Mari asked, sounding surprised.

"Yes, I do. Many times I have had to fix my clothes because I couldn't afford to buy new things," Peramal said as she took the dress from Ms. Mari's hand.

"OK, but please be careful; this is for one of our best customers. Her daughter is getting married Saturday. She came in for a fitting, and we have to move the buttons."

Peramal

Peramal worked on the dress all evening and finished it around midnight. She had to be extra careful. The dress was beautiful. She wished that someday she could have a wedding like this. That night she had a dream that she was wearing a beautiful white dress.

The next morning, Ms. Mari was very happy with her work. She told her that the store owner was looking for a person to work part-time and that maybe Peramal should apply for the job.

"Why don't you come with me, and I could tell Mr. Santiago and show him your work," Ms. Mari asked.

"But what about Julio? Shouldn't I ask him first?" Peramal asked with anxiety in her voice. Just then, Julio walked in the room.

"Ask me what?" Julio said, sounding annoyed. He had fallen in with the wrong crowd again. Most nights he was out partying and drinking, and probably doing drugs. He was angry all the time. Peramal sometimes was afraid that he would hit her if she antagonized him in some way.

Peramal spoke up first. "Your aunt said I did a great job sewing the buttons, and she thinks I could get a part-time job at her work."

"No," Julio responded as he grabbed a mug to pour himself some coffee. "I don't want you out there where other men can gawk at you!"

"But this is a great opportunity. I could make some mon—" before she had a chance to finish, Julio threw the mug at her, but she was able to dodge it; it hit the wall, shattering in tiny pieces, and hot coffee splattered everywhere.

"Julio! How dare you treat your wife like this!" Ms. Mari screamed at him. "If your mother, my sister, were here to see you like this, she would be disappointed!"

"Well, she is not! She's dead, and if you're not careful, you will be too!" Julio threatened his aunt and then stormed out of the house.

Peramal started to cry as she got down to the floor.

Ms. Mari tried to console her as they both cleaned up the broken glass. "I am so sorry, *mija*. He has never been this way before. It's the drugs making him do this."

Peramal kept crying.

"*Mira*, I am still going to show Mr. Santiago your work. I am sure he will be impressed and maybe he will let you do this work from home."

Peramal looked up and smiled through her tears, and Ms. Mari hugged her.

True to her word, Ms. Mari showed her boss the dress, and Mr. Santiago allowed Peramal to work on alterations from home. Ms. Mari taught her how to use a sewing machine, and she became a big help to her, especially when the arthritis in her fingers was acting up. Peramal was paid her fair share for the work, and she started to save up money. Peramal didn't tell her husband about it, because she knew he would get angry and probably take away the money to waste it on drugs and alcohol.

Julio would come home every night wasted. Most nights he would force himself on his young wife and would hit her if she refused. He would do it anyway, even though she repeatedly asked him to stop.

Peramal

It was almost Christmas, and Peramal was getting dressed. She found it difficult to zip up her pants. The weather had gotten a little colder, and she had to take out the only long pair of pants she had owned. She did not realize that she had gained that much weight. She had always been very thin, and she could eat anything she wanted without gaining an ounce.

As Julio walked in the room and grabbed her from behind, he noticed her struggle.

"Are you gaining weight? You better not be—I don't like my women chunky!" he said as he slapped her on the behind, grabbed his jacket, and left to meet his friends.

Distraught, she sat down, trying to figure out the dates in her head. Then she realized that it had been many weeks since her last period. With everything going on, she had completely forgotten about it. A wave of nausea overcame her, and she felt like she was about to throw up. Peramal ran to the bathroom and did just that.

"Oh no! I can't be pregnant!" she anxiously whispered to herself. "What am I going to do!"

"Peramal! Peramal!" she heard Ms. Mari calling. "Come! Have dinner with me. I made you your favorite, *arroz con pollo*!"

Just hearing the name of the food made Peramal nauseated again. The sickness hit her like a ton of bricks.

She walked into the kitchen with her had hand on her mouth and nose. Ms. Mari was scooping the rice onto the plate.

"Peramal, are you OK? You don't look so good!" her husband's aunt said, looking concerned.

She put the plate down and went to Peramal's side. "Come, sit down. You look pale, like you are going to pass out. Should I call the doctor?" the older women anxiously asked.

"No, no, I am OK," the younger girl said in a quiet voice. "I think I am pregnant."

Peramal held her breath not knowing how Ms. Mari would react.

"Oh my! How exciting!" Ms. Mari was filled joy and excitement as she hugged her.

"This is wonderful news! A *bambino*! Does Julio know yet?"

"Not yet. I just realized it now, but don't I have to take a test to be sure or go to the doctor?" Peramal asked.

"*Sí, sí*, I will take you to the doctor tomorrow to be sure and then you can tell him," Ms. Mari replied.

"Ms. Mari, do you think Julio is going to be mad and not want the baby?" Peramal asked.

"*Mija*, of course he'll want the baby!" Ms. Mari assured her, "Either way, it doesn't matter! I am here for you, and this baby is a true blessing!"

The next morning, Peramal and Ms. Mari went to the doctor, and sure enough, he confirmed that Peramal was about two months pregnant. Dr. Pérez gave her a checkup, and everything was fine. He gave her vitamins to take and told her that she needed to make sure to keep up with her appointments with him so that she could have a healthy baby.

That night, Peramal told Julio, and, Ms. Mari was right, he was excited on the prospect of having a son. But his auntie reminded him that there was a chance that it could be girl as well.

Julio had completely changed; he was very attentive. He had finally gotten a job, as a mechanic. Once again, Peramal was hopeful that things were going to get better.

It had been months since she had read the water, and she wanted to keep it that way. But she couldn't control her dreams. She wasn't getting much sleep because she was constantly dreaming about her grandmother—that she was gravely ill and she didn't have much time left. Peramal knew that she had to go and see her.

Peramal broached the subject with Julio, but he totally shut her down. At one point, when she wasn't backing down, he tried to strike her, but his aunt got in the way and stopped him. She reminded him that he could hurt his unborn child.

It was April, and she was seven months pregnant. Peramal was glowing and looked as beautiful as ever. Ms. Mari was helping her get ready for the baby. They were shopping for baby clothes at a children's boutique in the small downtown area of San Juan when Peramal noticed a woman, not that much older than her, staring at her. The young lady had two small children with her.

"Peramal?" the stranger asked in a soft voice.

Peramal was surprised that this stranger knew her name. "Yes, do I know you?" she asked hesitantly.

The young women smiled and said, "No, we never met, but I have seen your picture at my mother's house. I'm Katherine, Mrs. González's daughter."

"Oh! It's nice to meet you!" Peramal said. "Thank you for letting me borrow your dress!"

"It's nothing!" Katherine said. "I should be thanking you for the reading and your prayers for my two little miracles!"

"You don't have to thank me. They are beautiful! I am so happy for you," Peramal replied.

"I see that you have one on the way! Congratulations!" Katherine said to the expectant mother.

Peramal smiled shyly. "Oh, this is my husband's auntie, Ms. Mari," Peramal said making the introductions between the two women. They were exchanging greetings when Katherine's son knocked over a clothes rack.

"Oh no! I better go!" Katherine said. She picked up the clothes rack and then grabbed her son and put him in the stroller, where his sister was already strapped in. "We should get together sometime. Also, I don't know what you are having, but your welcome to the baby clothes that I have. Give me your number and I can call you?"

Ms. Mari reached in her purse, wrote the number down, and gave it to Katherine.

"I would love that! Thank you so much for the baby clothes!" Peramal said, hoping that she and Katherine would one day become good friends.

The next couple of months went by quickly and on her sixteenth birthday, Peramal gave birth to a beautiful, healthy baby boy. She named him Victor. Motherhood came naturally to her, and she felt like she had found the missing part of her that she had been searching for a long time. It was a magical feeling to love someone so much and to feel the unconditional love in return. Even when she was exhausted because of waking up several times during the night for feedings and changing diapers, just seeing that sweet smile from her son made her forget how tired she was.

Initially, Julio was overjoyed at having a son, but things changed quickly.

He didn't realize the responsibility and the long nights of interrupted sleep that come with the territory of parenthood. And the fact that now he had to share Peramal's attention made him even more angry, and he started to resent his son.

Ms. Mari, however, was a godsend to her. Even though Ms. Mari had never had children of her own, she had grown up in a household of ten kids. She knew a thing or two about taking care of a baby. She had helped take care of Julio when he was a baby too.

Victor was a very easy-going baby, which Peramal was extremely grateful for. There were times she feared for her son when he wouldn't stop crying because he had a cold and Julio would yell at him.

Victor was about three months old when the dreams about her grandmother started coming again. But this time, she also saw her aunt, Letti. They both showed up at her kitchen door drenched in water. Peramal was about to reach out to hug them when the sound of Victor's crying woke her up. Her arms were raised, midair. She realized it had been a dream, and now it was time for her son's feeding. Like clockwork, Victor would wake up at two thirty in morning—at least, he had been for the last few days since the dreams started up again.

Morning came with a torrential downpour; the sound of thunder bellowed and shook the house. Peramal went to check on Victor to make sure the sound hadn't scared him, but he was sleeping soundly. The next unexpected sound was a loud knock at the door. For a moment Peramal was excited and thought that it was her grandmother and auntie coming to see her, just like in her dream. But it was Katherine and her mother there instead.

"Mrs. González, it is so wonderful to see you again! I really missed you!" Peramal exclaimed. She was excited to see them but was also slightly disappointed that it was not her grandmother. Although she knew that her grandmother was not perfect and sometimes treated Peramal badly, Peramal wanted to make amends, because after all, her grandmother had taken her in when she was abandoned by her own mother.

"Come in, come in, please! Are you visiting for you a while?" She asked the older lady.

The floor got wet from the rain-drenched umbrellas and jackets. They apologized for making a mess and offered to clean it up, but Peramal told them not to worry as she grabbed a floor towel and took care of the water.

"Peramal, it is nice to see you too. I came on the bus this morning. Congratulations on the new baby," Mrs. González said, smiling, but that smile didn't reach her eyes; she looked sad.

"How about I make us some breakfast and coffee? Are you hungry?" Peramal said as she started working in the kitchen. "I just fed Victor and put him down for his morning nap."

"No, no, please don't do anything," Mrs. González said as she tried to get Peramal to sit down. "I need to tell you something important. "

"Are you alone? Is Ms. Mari here?" Katherine asked.

"No, no one is here. Ms. Mari doesn't like to drive in the rain, so Julio had to take her to work," Peramal answered.

Katherine took the younger girl by the hand, and she had her sit down at the kitchen table. Peramal felt a chill go through her body; she knew that it was something bad coming, and she didn't want to hear it. Even before a word was uttered, she knew that her grandmother and auntie had died.

"Your grandmother and auntie—they were driving home, and it was late and raining hard. Their car swerved and landed in a lake, and they couldn't get out," Katherine had to break the news to her because her mother became too emotional and couldn't get the words out.

Mrs. González was worried about Peramal. The poor girl has already been through so much.

Peramal sat there in stunned silence. Then a thought occurred to her, and she asked the question that she already knew the answer to. "Did this happen around two thirty this morning?

"Yes, it did. I am so sorry, Peramal," Katherine responded.

"I have a letter for you." Mrs. González finally found her voice. "Your grandmother heard about you living in San Juan when Katherine came home for a visit last month. Katherine told her about the baby. A couple of days before the accident, I mentioned to her that I was coming out this way if she wanted to join me, but she said that she couldn't—maybe next time. Instead she gave me this envelope."

Peramal took the letter, her hands shaking. She did not know what to expect. Her grandmother always appeared emotionally detached from everything, except when she had her moments of anger and she was beating Peramal. She was not exactly the loving type. Even when her son, Peramal's father, died, she remained stoic.

The young girl unfolded the paper and saw two simple words written in Spanish: "*Lo siento.*" Along with the paper, there was a torn empty envelope with her mother's name and a New York address. It was postmarked eight years ago.

"I'm sorry?" Peramal spoke in an angry, loud voice. "I'm sorry?" she repeated. "That is all she could say? Eight years of pain, eight years of claiming she did not know where my mother went, eight years of me wanting so desperately to find my mother, eight years of feeling abandoned and alone! And all I get is, *I'm sorry!*"

Peramal wasn't sure if she was angry and upset that her grandmother and aunt had died, or that her grandmother had kept her mother away from her for so long. It didn't matter. All of those emotions welled up inside of her and poured out in hysterical tears as she slid off the chair onto the floor, crying in anguish.

Chapter 7

Ms. Mari convinced Julio that they had to go and take Peramal so she could be there to take care of her grandmother and aunt's funeral. Julio didn't want to be bothered. He relented and told his wife that she could go, but she only had two weeks to come back; if she didn't comply with his request, he would chase her down, divorce her, and take away Victor, and she would never see her son again. The young girl knew that Julio was crazy enough that he would follow through with this threat.

Two days later, they left for Ponce. Mrs. González traveled back with them. She offered to take care of Victor while Ms. Mari looked after Peramal.

Peramal felt conflicted. Part of her wanted to go back and face her demons, and the other wanted to run away with her son and never look back.

It was midnight by the time the bus arrived at its destination. With the heavy rains, some of the roads were washed out, and the driver had to take several detours.

Everyone was relived they had made it safely.

"Here we are. Please come and stay with me. I have plenty of room, and I could watch Victor while you go and take care of everything in the morning. *¿Sí?*" Mrs. González offered. Peramal was grateful; she wasn't ready to face the demons, at least not that night.

"Thank you, Mrs. González," she answered with relief. "But are you sure that we won't be too much for you? We could go to my grandmother's place…" Her voice trailed off because she was hoping Mrs. González would insist on her house; thankfully, she did.

"Of course not! I love baby sounds in the house! It does my heart good! Come on in, Ms. Mari, welcome to my home," Mrs. González said as she went to unlock the front door.

Before going into the house, Peramal looked over to her grandmother's house next door. She stood transfixed. It looked dark and eerie. It didn't help that it was foggy and the moon was big and bright; it cast a shadow from the trees. A feeling of fear, violence, and dread overcame her, and she found it hard to breathe. She became hysterical.

Ms. Mari didn't realize that Peramal was still outside when she heard screams. She went to investigate the sound and saw the door was ajar. She stepped out to the porch to find the young girl on the floor, crying.

"Oh no! Oh no! They killed her! They killed her!" Peramal screamed over and over until she passed out.

The two older ladies got Peramal to bed so that she could sleep. They both prayed to God and the Virgin Mary to give her strength, to get through the next few days.

Peramal

The next morning, Peramal woke up and focused on the tasks at hand. It was like a switch had suddenly turned off and she couldn't feel a thing. There was a bassinet next to her bed, and she could see her son sleeping soundly. She may have turned off her emotions to the world, but her heart still held a special place for her son, and it melted every time she saw him. She kissed his forehead and made her way downstairs to the kitchen.

"*Buenos días*," the young girl greeted Mrs. González and Ms. Mari.

They were sitting at the table drinking coffee and were surprised to find the girl dressed and ready to go out. "Thank you for taking care of me last night. I am sorry if I was any trouble."

"No. No need to be sorry. Are you OK, *mija*?" Ms. Mari asked as got up to give her a hug.

"Can I get you some coffee and breakfast?" Mrs. González asked.

"I could take some black coffee, please. I am not hungry. I just want to go and get everything over with, if that is OK, Ms. Mari?" Peramal asked in a tired voice. She hadn't gotten get any sleep. As she was drinking the coffee, she said to Mrs. González, "Victor is still sleep. I put his formula in the refrigerator. He will probably sleep for another hour or so." She half-finished the hot liquid and then followed Ms. Mari outside.

The two women borrowed Mrs. González's car. The first stop was the police station. to find out where her grandmother and aunt's bodies were. The detective in charge informed her that the lake was too deep and filled with crocodiles, so it would be too difficult to pull the car out. The chances of finding the bodies were slim to none.

They took Peramal's information and told her if anything came up, they would contact her.

After the police station, they made their way to her grandmother's lawyer and sometimes bookkeeper, Marco Morales. She was not sure if her grandmother had recent contacts with him; it had been years since she had owned the restaurant and had required his legal services. Once again, they came up empty. Abuela did not have a penny to her name, and she never had a will drawn up, nor had she bought life insurance. The only thing that was of any value was her house. However, she did not even own that anymore. A month before she died, she had written a letter stating that she was giving her house to Don Carlo, a local businessman who owned half of the town. Marco gave her the letter to read.

Ms. Mari sat quietly next to Peramal, offering her support. But upon hearing that name, Don Carlo, Ms. Mari visibly flinched, like a knife was piercing her heart. Neither the lawyer nor Peramal noticed her reaction, and she was relieved. She put her own thoughts aside and decided to listen to what was going on around her.

"I am sorry for your loss, Ms. Otero. I know that this a lot to process," Mr. Morales spoke from behind his desk.

"But I don't understand; why would she do this?" Peramal asked, sounding incredibly confused.

"It is not my place to perpetuate rumors, but off the record, it was my understanding that she lost her house in a card game," the lawyer explained.

"I see. Thank you," she said as she got up to leave, but then she thought of another question. "Mr. Morales, do I have any time to go back to the house to get some things?"

"Actually, yes. You have about two more days. I am not sure if you noticed, but the later stated that you have seven days from date of your grandmother's death. Let me know if there is anything that I can do for you?"

"Thank you, Mr. Morales," Ms. Mari said as she put her arm around Peramal and guided her out of the lawyer's office.

Outside, the sun was shining over them, even though clouds were gathering in the distance. Peramal stopped, closed her eyes, and tilted her face up toward the sky, enjoying the warmth. She stood there for a minute, hoping that she would wake up from this nightmare.

"*Mija*, are you OK?" Ms. Mari asked with concern in her voice. "Come. Here's a bench. Let's sit down."

"So. We have accomplished nothing at this point. We are back where we started," the young girl stated in dejected voice. "What are we supposed to do? There is no closure. I don't care that there's no money; I just wanted to be able to say good-bye. I never had the chance with my father, nor with my mother, and now not with Abuela either. I don't know how or why I have to deal with this—I'm only sixteen years old!"

Ms. Mari gently cradled her face between her hands and spoke softly. "Listen to me, angel. I know that you have been through so much already. But life doesn't know age; it doesn't wait for anyone or anything, it just happens. It is how you handle it that will shape your future. You have a son, and he is your future. You need to focus on that. Now, we will go to the church and ask the priest if we could hold a memorial service. We will make sure that you can say your good-byes."

Peramal grabbed Ms. Mari, hugged her hard, and then said, "I don't know what I would do without you!"

Father Santos greeted them at the church. He had heard about her grandmother's passing and offered his condolences. Peramal loved going to church; it brought her a sense of peace and hope.

They agreed to have the memorial on Saturday morning. The priest suggested that she put a notice in the local newspaper so that people would know where to go to pay their respects.

Peramal used most of the money that she had saved from her work as a seamstress to pay for the notice and for some refreshments, to be served in the church hall after the memorial service.

Very few people showed up for her grandmother, and even less for her aunt. She was relieved that Cousin Alberto wasn't around. It was rumored that he had moved to New York and was living with Peramal's mother, but that was town gossip, and she had no time for that.

Father Santos had asked if she wanted to say anything at the service, but she declined. She couldn't bring her herself to talk about them when all she felt was resentment and anger.

She was doing her best to forgive them, but it was not going to happen overnight. Two lifetimes culminated in a half an hour of prayers for their souls, for forgiveness, and for everlasting peace, and then the service was over.

Peramal thanked everyone for coming and said her good-byes.

Ms. Mari was quiet on the drive back to Mrs. González's house. She kept thinking about what the lawyer had said about Don Carlo. It had been a long time since she heard that name.

"Ms. Mari? Ms. Mari? Are you OK?" Peramal asked with concern in her voice. "We're here. Don't you want to go inside?"

Ms. Mari was confused as she turned to look at the younger girl. For a moment she had forgotten where she was and what she was doing. Her hands gripped the steering wheel so tight that they started to ache.

"I'm sorry, *mija*. I guess I am a little tired," the older woman finally responded. "Let's go inside and see that little baby of yours, and then we can go tomorrow to your grandmother's house. We are both too exhausted to have to deal with that today."

Peramal agreed.

Mrs. González had dinner waiting for them. Victor was in the bassinet, smiling and content, making the sweetest sounds of cooing and gurgling. His mother bent down to kiss him on cheek and take in that wonderful baby smell.

"Peramal, come and eat." Mrs. González invited her to the table, where Ms. Mari was already seated.

The ladies finished their dinner and everyone helped clear the table and wash the dishes. No one sat down until everything was done. Peramal made the coffee, and then they went and sat on the porch, discussing the day's events.

Peramal was coming to terms with everything and trying to move on and make peace with it. But there was still a part of her that gnawed at her, telling her that something bad was going to happen. She tried to put it out of her mind.

Without thinking about it—she didn't know why she was even asking—she offered to read the water for Ms. Mari. "Ms. Mari, how about I read the water for you? You have done so much for me, and you never once asked me to read for you? Is there anything that I could help you with?"

Peramal caught her by surprise, so much that she almost spilled the cup of coffee in her hand.

"¡Sí, sí!, you should try it, our Peramal is so good at it!" Mrs. González encouraged her.

"Thank you, Peramal. I'm OK, and it's getting late and we have a busy day tomorrow. Oh! I think I hear Victor crying," Ms. Mari said, without even waiting for a response as she rushed into the house.

That night Peramal was restless and experienced very vivid dreams, but she could only remember one that stayed with her and that she didn't want to forget.

She saw her grandmother standing in the middle of the kitchen. She was drenched and extremely pale, and her eyes were dark, sunken in the sockets. In her hand she was carrying a Bible; it was Peramal's father Bible, written in

Spanish. She knew that Bible well. Her father would read from it every night when he was home, and Peramal would sit with him. The Bible was special to her, but her grandmother had taken it from Peramal and kept it after he died. In the dream her grandmother was mumbling in gibberish as she was trying to give her the Bible. As Peramal reached for it, her grandmother dropped it in a pot of boiling water, and it started to disintegrate. Peramal screamed and put her had in the water, the heat burning and blistered her skin, but she didn't care; she wanted her father's Bible. Then, the sound of Victor's crying woke her up, and she found herself on the floor.

She got up and took care of Victor. After that, she headed downstairs with Victor in her arms, only to find Mrs. González coming up the stairs.

"Good morning, Peramal," the older woman said. "Did you sleep well? Come, give me the bambino and go take are shower so you could get some breakfast. Ms. Mari is downstairs already."

"Thank you, Mrs. González. I will be down as soon as I can," Peramal replied.

About an hour later, Ms. Mari and Peramal walked over to the house next door. Not a word was spoken about what had happened the night before.

As they climbed up the steps of the porch, they noticed the door was slightly ajar, and a feeling of dread overcame them. "Could there be someone inside?" Ms. Mari whispered, with fear in her voice. "Maybe we should call the police!"

"I don't think so now, but I think someone was here looking for something," Peramal spoke as she pushed open the door.

"Wait, mija!" Ms. Mari implored the young girl, but Peramal didn't wait and went on in the house. Ms. Mari closely followed her.

The house was a mess. Everything was turned upside down, with glass broken and furniture torn up. Someone had really done a number on the place.

"*¡Ay, Dios mío!*" Ms. Mari exclaimed while trying to stay as quiet as possible; she was still afraid someone was still there.

"Do you think they found what they were looking for?" the older woman asked as they started walking for room to room.

"No, they didn't. But we better hurry; I think they will be coming back soon," Peramal warned. "I only want to find a couple of things: my doll from when I was a little girl and my papa's Bible."

They searched the entire house and finally found Peramal's doll. But that too was damaged and ripped apart. Peramal looked sad as she inspected the doll.

"Don't worry, we can fix it." Ms. Mari tried to comfort the younger girl.

"But, where can the Bible be?" Peramal spoke in frustration. "We looked everywhere." Then it hit her—the dream.

"The kitchen!" the younger girl exclaimed as she walked toward the kitchen. Ms. Mari followed her, feeling confused.

The kitchen looked like a tornado had traveled through it. All of the contents of the cabinets were cleared out and sitting on the floor, including the pots and pans. Flour, rice, and spices had been poured out of their containers. Her grandmother had kept most of the kitchen supplies from when she owned the restaurant.

Once again, Peramal was disappointed. They didn't find the Bible. She sat down, lost in thought, trying to figure out if her grandmother was trying to tell her something.

"Maybe we should leave. I am afraid they might be coming back. Look at those shelves up there. They haven't been touched. You know they will come back," Ms. Mari spoke as she pointed to the shelf above the refrigerator.

Peramal was hopeful again. She put one chair on top of another and climbed up. There it was, among the cookbooks piled on the shelf. Along with the Bible, there was a stack of letters tied together. The letters were addressed to her grandmother, with the postmark from New York. Peramal grabbed them and the Bible and climbed down, but not before she noticed that there was a hand gun top of the refrigerator, covered by a layer of dust.

"There is a gun up here. Should I bring it down?"

"Yes, but be careful where you point it."

Peramal gave Ms. Mari the Bible and letters, and then she grabbed the gun and handed to her as well. Ms. Mari looked at it to make sure the safety lock was on.

"Did you know that your grandmother had a gun?"

"No, I didn't. What should we do with it? Give it to the police?"

"Yes, I think we should." They took the Bible and letters and place them in a bag, while Ms. Mari put the gun in her pocket.

"Are you ready to go?" Ms. Mari asked.

"Yes, please." Peramal responded. She just wanted to leave and put all of this behind her.

"OK, let's go. Did you want to take anything else with you? Maybe some pictures? If you can find any," Ms. Mari suggested.

Peramal nodded and found some pictures strewn all over the floor. It was hard to find one picture of her whole family together, because there wasn't much of an opportunity for one to be taken with her father away so often.

They grabbed their stuff, including the gun, and made their way out of Abuela's house. A few seconds later, the two women heard a car drive up behind them and turn into the driveway of Peramal's grandmother's house. The car was dark, with tinted windows. Two men dressed in black stepped out of the vehicle and went into the house, without paying any attention to the women walking along the sidewalk.

Ms. Mari and Peramal hurried away and didn't stop until they got to Mrs. González's house. They never looked back.

Chapter 8

Three years had passed since that day at her grandmother's house. Peramal took the Bible and stuck the letters in it; then she hid it where no one could find it. She knew those letters were important; why else would her grandmother try and hide them like that? She wanted to read them, but she never could find the time alone to be able to do that. It felt like Julio was her shadow; she could never go anywhere or do anything without him being within five feet of her.

They had settled in a routine, but Julio seemed to struggle with his demons. He was like Dr. Jekyll and Mr. Hyde; Peramal did not know who to expect when he came home every evening. Sometimes he was sweet and playful, and other times he was abusive and angry enough that he threatened to kill her. She knew that if Ms. Mari wasn't around, he would actually go through with it. In the back of her mind, she knew that someday she would have no choice but to leave.

On the morning of Victor's fourth and her twentieth birthday, she woke up to a wave of nausea when she sat up. She felt so sick that she had to lie back down again to wait for it to pass.

Julio was sound asleep next to her; he had been out drinking all night again.

Peramal willed herself to get up again. She had so much to do to get ready for Victor's birthday party. She had invited some of the kids from his preschool to come over for some cake and ice cream, and perhaps to play a few games. Before going downstairs, she checked on Victor, who was still sleeping. *He looks like a little angel*, she thought to herself and was grateful he was in her life.

"Happy birthday, Peramal! Is the birthday boy still sleeping? I can't believe he is already four years old!" Ms. Mari greeted her. "Wait, you don't look so good, *mija*. Are you feeling sick? You look really pale."

"Yes, I don't feel so good either," she answered.

"Come, sit down." Ms. Mari said as she pulled out a chair for her. "Do you think you have the flu? I know something is going around."

"No. I think I am pregnant." Peramal said in a quiet voice. She had always wanted a sibling for Victor. But things have not been going well with Julio recently; he'd been very unstable. He had become extremely paranoid and was always accusing her of cheating on him.

"Oh, how exciting! What a wonderful birthday gift!" Ms. Mari said excitedly. "A new baby!" Then the older woman realized that something was wrong. "Aren't you happy?"

"Of course I'm happy. I'm just afraid that right now, things are so unstable with the way Julio has been acting," the younger girl explained.

"It doesn't matter. If there is a baby coming, we will welcome it and be grateful!" Ms. Mari comforted her.

❖

It was noon, time for the birthday party. There were only six children that showed up along with their parents. Katherine and her two children came as well. Julio was still sleeping off the night of drinking—under no circumstances did he want anyone to wake him up, even for his son's birthday party. Peramal set up a table outside in the yard, on the opposite side of the house from where Julio was sleeping. But Julio could still hear the noise, and it woke him up.

"What is that noise? Peramal! Peramal!" he yelled angrily as he got up, stomping like a madman throughout the house looking for his wife. He had a splitting headache, and the noise was making it worse. "I have a headache! I need something for it! Would someone turn off that noise!" He got angrier when there was no response. He went outside to investigate and he saw his wife talking and laughing with a man—the only man that had showed up with his daughter. Julio's paranoia got the best of him, and he was convinced that she was talking and laughing about him. He was also convinced that she was sleeping with that man.

Julio charged toward them, turning over the table with the cake and food. The kids ran away, crying to their parents. Then he punched the man that was talking to Peramal, and he grabbed her arm, pulling her inside the house. She tripped along the way, and he started to drag her. Ms. Mari tried to stop him, but he was too strong for her and pushed her away. Once inside, Julio started to repeatedly punch her in the face and stomach. He only stopped when Peramal became limp and collapsed to the floor—blood seeping beneath her. He was about to raise his fist again to go in for another blow, but he stopped in midair when a moment of clarity hit him like a ton of bricks. It was like he was watching himself outside his body, and he couldn't believe what he just had done to his wife. He panicked and ran out of the house.

❧

Peramal was rushed to the hospital and treated for her injuries. But they couldn't do anything to save the baby. One of the parents from the party had called the police, and Julio was taken into custody. They found him hiding underneath Ms. Mari's house.

The police showed up at the hospital and asked Peramal if she wanted to press charges. She declined. She explained to them that her husband has been under a lot of stress and that he had never done anything like this before. One of the detectives gave her his card and asked to call if she changed her mind.

"You should have pressed charges, *mija*!" Ms. Mari said, frustrated. "I know he is my nephew, but he needs help! Maybe spending time in jail will teach him a lesson!"

"I can't! It would only make things worse for me! I can't go anywhere, he will chase me down! I don't care what happens to me; I just don't want him hurting Victor!" Peramal cried. The two women hugged each other and cried over the loss of the baby.

The young mother was released from the hospital two days later. Ms. Mari picked her up and took her home. Julio was nowhere to be found.

"Mama! Mama! You're home!" Victor cried happily as he ran to her once she got home from the hospital. Mrs. González had been watching him. She had heard what happened from her daughter and wanted to come and help if she could.

"Oh, you poor girl, are you OK? I am so sorry," Mrs. González said as she hugged her close.

They all went into the house to get Peramal settled in. Mrs. González stayed about a week. Ms. Mari needed the extra help because she was very busy at the dress shop, and it was difficult for her to manage while taking care of Peramal and Victor.

Peramal was feeling much better and thanked her for her kindness, but she didn't want to impose on her any longer. Mrs. González went on her way back home.

It was a hot July afternoon about a month after the attack, and Victor was watching TV while Peramal sat at the kitchen table mending a dress for Mr. Santigo's customer. The whirling sound of the fan was so loud that it was the only noise she could hear.

She was so engrossed in the stitching that she didn't realize someone had walked in the kitchen. A hand gripped her on the shoulder, and she jumped up out of her chair, knocking over the fan. It was Julio. This the first time she had seen him since the birthday party. His eyes were bloodshot and his clothes wrinkled, and it looked had not shaved for days.

She was afraid of him, but she tried not to show it. Her heart was racing, and all she could think about was how she might defend herself. She noticed that there was a pair of scissors on the counter and tried subtly to edge her way close to it, so that she could grab it behind from her back.

"Peramal, I'm sorry. I didn't mean to hurt you," he apologized in a whispered voice. "I don't know what happened. I promise that I will never do it again. I love you!"

He reached out for her and hugged her, and she dropped the scissors, keeping her hands to her side. She wanted so badly to believe him.

"Please don't leave me," he said as he started to cry. Then, his hands started to pull at her clothes and he started to kiss her, but he wasn't gentle. He wanted to prove a point: that she belonged to him and that he owned her.

He dragged her to the floor and while his hand had her arms pinned above her head, he pulled down her underwear and unzipped his pants.

"No! No! Please don't! Not now! Victor is in the next room!" she cried, trying to pushing him off of her. But it was no use; he took what was his and he didn't stop until he finished.

He got up off of the kitchen floor, adjusted his pants, and walked out without a word.

She sat in stunned silence; she looked over to see that luckily, Victor had fallen asleep. As she tried to get up, she doubled over in pain when she started to cramp. That was how Ms. Mari found her when she got home.

"Peramal! I'm home!" Ms. Mari said cheerfully as she walked in the door. Then she looked down to see Peramal on the floor. She realized what had happened without Peramal having to say a word.

In the days that followed, Peramal realized that she that had to play the game of survival. She needed to be two steps ahead of Julio. When he wanted her, she didn't fight it—it hurt less that way. When he was around, she was always within his eyesight, so he knew that she was there. He constantly needed attention or his ego stroked. But it was exhausting, and she constantly felt like she was walking on eggshells.

❖

Two years passed this way, and Peramal found herself pregnant again. She wasn't sure if she could ever get pregnant again, considering what had happened the last time. But she promised herself that she would not let anything happen to this baby. When she shared the news with Julio, he seemed happy about it. As long as his needs were met, he didn't care what was happening around him.

He couldn't hang on to a job longer than a month, and he was running out of places to find employment. Ms. Mari carried the burden of paying for everything in the household. Peramal tried to give her the money she made, but Ms. Mari refused; she wanted her to save it for a rainy day.

Peramal had not been experiencing many dreams; frankly, she was too tired because of caring for her son and the house to do so.

It was a beautiful Saturday evening in October, with Halloween right around the corner—along with Peramal's due date. The women were sitting on the porch watching Victor as he played with his friends in the yard.

"So, my love, what do you think you are having this time?" Ms. Mari asked the younger girl.

"I think it is a girl, or maybe I am hoping it is," Peramal said as she smiled, imagining the fun she would have dressing her little girl in pretty dresses and bows.

"I hope so too!" The older woman clapped her hands together with excitement and then asked, "Have you thought of a name?"

"No, not yet. Julio doesn't like any of the ones that I thought of," the young mother replied. "Do you like any names?" Then she remembered that Ms. Mari wasn't able to have children of her own, and she felt bad for asking her.

"I'm sorry, Ms. Mari. I hope I didn't hurt your feelings," Peramal said apologetically.

"Oh, that's OK, *mija*, that was a long time ago. Besides, you are like the daughter that I never had, and if you don't mind me saying, your children are like grandchildren to me!"

Peramal was relieved. She smiled and then said, "So tell me, what names do you like? I really want to know, please?"

"I always loved the name Roberto, if it is a boy, and Melinda, if it is a girl. What do you think?" Ms. Mari asked.

"Oh, those are wonderful names! I would love to have a daughter named Melinda!" Peramal said excitedly. Two weeks later, on November 1, All Saints Day, Peramal got her wish: Melinda was born, healthy and beautiful.

Chapter 9

"It's back," Dr. Eric Ruiz spoke in a quiet voice as he sat perched on his desk, in front of the chair where Ms. Mari was sitting. He had a serious look on his face, and he wanted nothing more than to reach over and give her a hug. But he couldn't; if he did, he would fall apart, and he needed to be strong for her. They had been high school sweethearts, but life took them in different directions, and they married other people. They had always stayed in touch, especially when Ms. Mari had initially been diagnosed with breast cancer and he became her oncologist. Now, ten years later, he was delivering bad news again. But this time it was worse—the cancer had metastasized to the bones.

Dr. Ruiz had recently been divorced, and he never had any children. After the divorce, he had reconnected with Ms. Mari and had been planning a future with her. But now he wasn't sure how much of a future she had left. Whatever that future might be, he already knew that he would be there for her.

"How bad is it this time?" Ms. Mari asked, trying to keep her composure.

"It doesn't look good, *mi corazón*. It is very aggressive this time," Dr. Ruiz replied, trying to hold back his own tears. She was

Peramal

the love of his life, and he wasn't about to let her go without a fight. "We can fight this! There are new treatments that have recently been approved, and there is experimental therapy. I will do whatever it takes. We can beat this!" He tried to be encouraging.

"No. I don't want any treatment, *mi amor*, especially if there is no guarantee. There is no point. I would rather just live the life that I have left with you, Peramal, and the kids—not in a cold hospital getting poison put in my veins," Ms. Mari said, trying to be brave and sensible.

Eric couldn't stand it much longer. He didn't hold back the tears that came pouring out as he fell to his knees and hugged Mari so tightly that it was hard to breathe. But she didn't care; she was hanging onto him for dear life.

❖

Peramal had just finished feeding Melinda and putting her down for down for her late-morning nap. She had a few hours before she had to go pick up Victor from school. She couldn't believe that Melinda was almost two already; it seemed like yesterday that she was born.

Julio would be back next month, and she was hoping that he had saved some of the money that he was making. He had taken a three-month job on an oil rig in the Gulf of Mexico. Part of her was enjoying the freedom that she felt when he wasn't around, but she put that out of her mind, because she felt guilty for feeling that way.

The clock started to ring; it was eleven o'clock. She was waiting for Ms. Mari to come home from her doctor's appointment with Dr. Ruiz. She was hoping that it was a social visit—they had been spending a lot of time together, and Peramal had never seen Ms. Mari so happy. But Peramal had a nagging feeling that something was wrong, though she could never figure out what it was. She wanted to help, but Ms. Mari had refused whenever she offered to read the water for her. That was one thing about her gift that she couldn't control: if someone didn't open himself or herself up mentally, she wasn't able to read that person. But Peramal's dreams added to her anxiety. She kept seeing Ms. Mari on a boat, and she was drifting further away from her until she disappeared into a fog. Oftentimes, Peramal would wake up calling out Ms. Mari's name.

Ms. Mari finally got home at noon.

"Hola, Ms. Mari," Peramal greeted her and got up to give her a kiss on the cheek. "How was your morning? Did you see that handsome doctor? Did you want some lunch?" Peramal rambled on because she knew that she was going to hear something that she didn't like.

Ms. Mari walked silently to the cabinet and got a clear glass and filled it with water. The she took it to the table and sat down with the glass in front of her.

"*Mija*, would you read for me, please?" Ms. Mari asked in a soft voice, looking up at Peramal with tears in her eyes.

Peramal stood frozen. She was so afraid to move. "I can't. I can't...I'm afraid," she said, her voice barely a whisper.

"Please, *mija*. I need to know if you could tell me anything," Ms. Mari implored. Then she got up and took Peramal by the hand and led her to the table to sit before the glass.

The young girl was shaking, her face pale, her hands cold and clammy. She forced herself to do the reading.

"OK, put your hand on top of the glass, and I will cover it with mine," she instructed Ms. Mari. Then she closed her eyes and prayed really hard that Ms. Mari was going to be OK. Both women removed their hands off the glass, and Peramal picked it up to look to see if she saw any images.

"Dr. Ruiz really loves you. He wants to marry you," Peramal said with a smile. "He is a really good person."

Ms. Mari smiled too and blushed. She was happy to hear that.

Then Peramal looked beyond the happiness and found darkness and death. She couldn't bring herself to speak. She quickly stood up; the chair fell over, backward, and she ran out of the room crying, without saying a word. She closed the door to her room, threw herself on the bed, and covered her head with the blankets. She didn't want to face the truth that Ms. Mari was dying and she couldn't do anything to help her. *Why, God? Why do you want to take such a good person away! She doesn't deserve this! I need her! I can't do this by myself! Please God, save her!* Peramal cried in anguish as she silently prayed to God, the Virgin Mary, St. George, and all the angels and saints, or anyone in the heavens above that would listen to her.

❖

Ms. Mari sat at the kitchen table staring down the empty hallway. She didn't go after Peramal. She felt bad that she had put her in that situation, but she didn't have a choice because she knew that she didn't have much time left. Her thoughts were interrupted by a knock at the door; it was Eric. She opened the door to find him there, holding a bouquet of her favorite flowers, pink roses.

Ms. Mari was so happy to see him, and she reached out to hug him.

"Oh, Eric, I am so glad you are here," Mari said with relief and tears in her eyes.

"Are you OK, my love? Does something hurt?" Dr. Ruiz asked with concern in his voice.

"No, no. I'm OK. I'm upset about Peramal and I don't know what to do. How am I going get through this? I know I don't want treatment—but how long do I have? Who is going to help Peramal when I am gone? Julio is back next month, and he is unpredictable…he could hurt her!" Mari spoke with fear and anxiety in her voice.

"Take a deep breath, *mi amor*. Let's take this one day at a time; we will figure it out," Eric tried to reassure her. "But I have something important to tell you and to ask you."

Eric took Mari by the hand and led her to the couch in the sitting room.

They both sat down in silence for a minute or two. Eric felt very nervous, and he wasn't sure how to start, so he got down on one knee.

"I can't wait another minute longer. You are the love of my life, and I want nothing more than to be with you. Would you please marry me?"

Peramal

"*Mi corazón*, I love you more than anything, but I can't let you sacrifice your future for me when I don't have much of one," Ms. Mari said with tears running down her face as Eric held her.

"How can it be a sacrifice when you want to be with the person that you love most in this world? Please say you will marry me!" Eric asked once more.

❖

The silence of the bedroom was broken by a sweet voice saying, "Mama! Mama!" Peramal heard the sound of her daughter and removed the blankets that were on top of her head. Melinda had woken up from her nap and was standing up in her crib. The child opened up her arms, indicating that she wanted to be picked up.

"Hello, sweet baby girl. Did you have a good nap?" Peramal said as she got up from her bed to pick up the baby. She hugged her, taking in that wonderful scent, and she enjoyed that moment of happiness. "Let's go see what Abuelita is doing, and then we have to go pick up your brother from school. OK?" Melinda just laughed and gurgled as her mother kissed her cheeks.

As she walked down the hall toward the sitting room, she heard a male voice along with Ms. Mari's. It was Dr. Ruiz. He stood up as soon as Peramal entered the room, and he greeted her with a warm smile. He was very tall, probably over six feet as he towered over Peramal's five-foot-five-inch frame. His face was very handsome despite being slightly weathered by age. He had dark hair mixed with gray, giving it the salt-and-pepper look.

"Hello, Peramal. It's nice to see you again," Dr. Ruiz said as he bent down to give Peramal a peck on the cheek. "Hello, little princess! Do you remember me?" he spoke to Melinda as she reached out to him, smiling and laughing.

"Go! Up!" Melinda said that she wanted him to throw her up in the air and catch her.

Eric looked at Peramal to get her permission. "Oh, she remembers me! Peramal, is that OK?" Peramal nodded, and Melinda threw herself into his waiting arms.

Peramal then turned her attention to Ms. Mari and sat down next to her.

"I am so sorry, Ms. Mari. I shouldn't have run out on you! I just couldn't handle the thought of losing you!" Peramal apologized as her eyes started to tear up.

"That's OK, *mija*. I understand. I shouldn't have asked you to do that. I should be apologizing to you," Ms. Mari said as she reached over to hug Peramal.

"No! No! You don't have too!" Peramal said as she wiped the tears from her face.

"Eric and I have been talking, and we have made some plans. Maybe we could sit down later after dinner to talk about them. I really need to have your blessing. You are like a daughter to me." Ms. Mari said, trying hard not to cry. Peramal couldn't speak; she just nodded in agreement. The clock rang three o'clock, and it was time to pick up Victor from school.

"I'd better get ready to go. Would you watch Melinda for me? I don't think that I would be able to tear her away since she is having so much fun with Dr. Ruiz." The young mother said with a half smile as she left to pick up her son.

That evening, the three of them sat together, and Ms. Mari shared the good news. She and Dr. Ruiz were getting married. Peramal was really excited but sad at the same time—it was a bittersweet moment. Dr. Ruiz was also selling his practice; he planned to invest the money accordingly so that he could retire. He wanted to be able to spend as much time as he could with Mari, and perhaps they could do some traveling as well. Mari had always wanted to go to the Galapagos Islands in Peru, or perhaps to Ayers Rock in Australia. She had seen documentaries on the National Geographic channel and had always dreamed of going there.

The next few weeks was a flurry of activities as they got ready for the wedding. Ms. Mari wanted a small, simple ceremony where she was surrounded by the people she loved.

With Ms. Mari leaving, Peramal was concerned about money and where they would live. But, Ms. Mari assured her that they could continue to live in her house. Although that was a help, Peramal was concerned about the monthly living expenses. Ms. Mari was the one that carried the weight on her shoulders, and now Peramal had to take that on because with his track record, Julio was not very responsible. He was not going to have a choice; he would have to let her go out and work. *Maybe I could take over as the seamstress at Mr. Santiago's?* she thought to her herself as she was cooking dinner. Just the idea taking on the responsibility, going to a job every day, and really making her own money was an exciting thought.

Julio was coming home in a week. With everything going on, she knew that with all of these changes were going to set him off. She already felt like she was living with a ticking time bomb.

Just then the phone rang, interrupting her thoughts.

"Come pick me up; I am at the bus station." A voice in a harsh monotone spoke at the other end. There was so much street noise that she couldn't recognize the voice.

"Who is this?" she asked hesitantly.

"Who do you think it is? It's your husband! You already forgot about me?" The voice got angrier.

"Julio, I am sorry! It is hard to hear with all the noise in the background. I thought that you were coming in a week. Are you OK?" Peramal asked with fear and anxiety welling up inside her. She was already bracing her herself for the abuse. It had been a glorious and peaceful three months, but that was coming to an end, sooner than she expected. Something had gone wrong, and he wasn't going back to this job. Every fiber in her being was telling her that she had to run away. But she didn't listen to that voice.

"Just get down here!" He yelled at her before hanging up the phone without saying another word.

Chapter 10

It was a cold, crisp Saturday morning in November when Ms. Mari and Dr. Ruiz said their I-dos. Melinda was as adorable as ever as the flower girl; she was doing the best that any two-year-old would be able to do in an occasion like this. Victor was very handsome in a suit, and he served as the best man and ring bearer, while Peramal was the maid of honor.

Julio wanted no part in the event and mainly stayed quiet and in his own little world. But at night it was a different story. He repeatedly and violently forced himself on his wife, sometimes leaving bruises all over her body. Peramal kept quiet and covered up the lesions and put on a brave front. She didn't want Ms. Mari to worry about her and give her added stress. Dr. Ruiz tried to engage in conversation with Julio, to get to know him better, but Julio would shut him down and walk away.

The following Sunday, the week after the wedding, Mari and Eric were getting ready for their trip to Australia. It was summer there, so it would be a perfect time to go. Mari was starting to show signs of discomfort and slowing down, and they didn't want to wait much longer before taking a trip. They finished packing that morning; later in the day, they decided to stop by to see Peramal and the kids and talk to Julio about Peramal taking over Mari's job as the seamstress. Peramal had asked for their help because she was afraid to be alone with him when she asked.

When they arrived, Julio was still asleep, so they sat down and had coffee and spent time with the kids.

"Abuelo, can you help me with this math problem?" asked Victor as he came to sit next to Eric at the kitchen table. Peramal and Ms. Mari held their breath and looked at each other. They weren't sure how Dr. Ruiz would take that. It came naturally for the kids to see Ms. Mari as their surrogate grandmother, but they'd never discussed how Dr. Ruiz felt about his role as their surrogate grandfather.

Eric looked surprised at first, and then he beamed. "Abuelo," he repeated softly. "I love the sound of that."

He looked at Mari and Peramal gave them a wink; then he put his reading glasses on and said proudly, "Well, let's see how Abuelo can you help you."

There was a collective sigh of relief, and all seemed right with world—until Julio woke up and came into the kitchen, looking disheveled, with bloodshot eyes.

He grabbed a mug, poured himself some coffee, and sat at the kitchen table, where Victor and Eric were sitting. Melinda ran over to him to give her father a hug, but he pushed her away. He had hardly spent any time with his kids since he'd come back; he appeared to not want to have anything to do with them. Eric had finished helping Victor with the problem, so it was time to talk with Julio about the seamstress job.

Peramal spoke up first. "Victor, please take your sister and watch TV; we have something to discuss with your father." She wanted to be the one to do the asking, in case Julio got violent.

The kids left the kitchen, and Peramal, along with Ms. Mari, sat at the table.

"Since Ms. Mari cannot work much longer and they will be leaving the country for a little while, I thought it might be a good idea for me to take over job at the dress shop for now. We will need the money to take of care the expenses. Please, Julio, don't get angry. I am only doing this to help take care of our family."

Peramal started to ramble on because she was so nervous. She wanted to present it as a temporary situation initially and then hopefully, it would work itself out. Even though he had been told about Ms. Mari's health condition, Julio didn't seem to comprehend the gravity of the situation.

Sitting at the table, Julio started to get agitated; he clenched his fists. He looked like he was about to throw the coffee mug at someone, but thankfully, he didn't. He knew Peramal was right. He hasn't been able to find or even keep a job. He had gotten into a fight on the oil rig with the supervisor; needless to say, he would never be allowed to go back.

"OK, but you go straight there and come straight home, you hear me," Julio said with controlled anger and then stormed out of the kitchen.

Ms. Mari turned to her husband and, in a hushed voice, said, "I am not so sure that we should leave, *mi amor*. I am so afraid for Peramal and the kids."

Dr. Ruiz agreed with his wife and said, "Listen, I can cover your expenses so you don't have to work until we come back in about a month, and then we can figure it out from there."

"That is very generous of you, Dr. Ruiz, and I appreciate it from the bottom of my heart. But I can't. I think it will make him angrier, and that is not what I need right now. Please, go on your trip. I have learned to handle him. I will be OK. He's changing," she tried to reassure them. "You have already done so much for me."

Every ounce of her being wanted to tell them to stay, but that would be selfish of her. It was time for her to overcome her insecurities and stand up for herself. She was constantly leaning on Ms. Mari, and that had to stop.

The next day, they said their final good-byes. It was the hardest thing Peramal ever had to do. Even when her mother had left her when she was eight years old, it did not compare to the pain that she was experiencing now. She felt like her heart was going to burst.

"Peramal, take this business card. It is for my lawyer. If you need anything, please call him. He will be able to get a hold of us in an emergency," Dr. Ruiz explained.

"I don't want to bother you. I will be OK," said Peramal as she tried to give him the card back.

"*Mija*, please take it. It will make me feel better about leaving you," Ms. Mari implored.

Peramal finally agreed. Ms. Mari and Dr. Ruiz said their good-byes to the children, and then got in the car and drove away.

Victor took Melinda inside the house while Peramal stayed out on the porch to get her head together. She pulled out the card out of her pocket to look at it when she was startled by sound. It was Julio walking up the steps. He came over to her and grabbed the card from her hand.

"Who is this? Your lover? Were you with him while I was gone? Answer me, you whore!" Julio screamed at her in a jealous rage.

"No! Of course!" Peramal cried back. "Give the card back to me!"

But that angered him even more. Instead of doing that, Julio slapped her across the face and tore up the business card in tiny little pieces. Then he grabbed her by hair and pulled her into the house. He threw her to floor and got on top of her. She knew what was coming next.

"Victor! Take your sister and go to your room! Now!" She yelled at her son who stood frozen, not knowing what to do. Victor hesitated at first and then picked up his sister and ran to his room, slamming the door.

Peramal tried to fight him off, but he repeatedly punched her in the face, and then he tried to choke her. She passed out for few seconds and woke up feeling pain and pressure as he was raping her.

When he finished, he got up and walked away, but not before he said, "If you ever try and leave me or even look at another man, I will kill you and the kids, and that is a promise."

Peramal knew that was not an empty threat. At that moment, she realized that she'd had enough. She had to plan an escape.

Chapter 11

"You are doing a beautiful job, Peramal, and the customers love you. They only want *you* to work on their clothes!" Mr. Santiago complimented her. "I was sorry to see Ms. Mari leave, but, I am so happy to have you in her place."

"*De nada*," Peramal replied, feeling a little shy and awkward. She wasn't used to this kind of attention. Most of her life, she had been belittled and treated poorly.

It had been three months since she took over for Ms. Mari. So far she had been able to manage with the kids and the house. Most nights, she was barely getting five hours of sleep. She had to make sure that the cooking, cleaning, and laundry were done so Julio had no reason to complain. Thankfully, she was able to find a church near the dress shop that had a day care for Melinda and where Victor could go when he didn't have school. Although she could barely afford it, she needed a place where she could trust that they would be safe. With the added expense, she knew that it would take years to save up enough money to get out. But she had no choice. Julio spent most of time hanging out with the wrong crowd, and not much else.

He didn't even try to find a job. What kept her going was that she had a plan: someday, somehow she was going to escape.

It was almost noon, and Peramal was getting up to take her lunch break and went to the front of the shop. Just then, the door opened, and Katherine walked in. Peramal couldn't remember the last time she had seen her. They had lost touch after that birthday party, when Julio made it difficult for her to carry on any kind of friendship with anyone. Even when he was on the oil rig, it felt like he had this invisible hold on her—and he still did now.

"Katherine! *¡Hola!* How are you?" Peramal greeted her old friend.

"Peramal! Is that you? I can't believe it!" Katherine exclaimed as she reached out to hug her. "Do you work here?"

"Yes, I do, and I was just about to take my lunch break. If you have time, we can catch up and go to the coffee shop next door?"

"I would love to!"

"I'm sorry. I just realized you probably came here to get something. I didn't mean to interrupt your plans," Peramal said apologetically.

"Oh no! That's OK. I was in the area and wanted to check out dresses. My cousin is getting married next month," Katherine explained.

"OK, then let's go get some lunch, and then I can help find a dress. You will look beautiful!" Peramal said excitedly and then said to her boss, "Mr. Santiago, I am going on my lunch break."

"Of course," he replied and then added, "take your time. Enjoy. You hardly ever take one." He smiled and then went back to organizing the display case.

The two women made their way next door, where they sat at a table by the window. The waitress came to take their order for a couple of lemonades and sandwiches. Once the started talking, they couldn't stop. *It's so nice to be able to just let go and enjoy myself, and forget about my worries*, Peramal thought to herself. She didn't remember the last time she was able to do this.

Peramal filled Katherine in on her kids and on how well they were doing, and then about Ms. Mari and Dr. Ruiz getting married. Katherine started to tear up when she heard the news about Ms. Mari's health.

"I'm sorry, Katherine. I didn't mean to upset you." Peramal tried to console her as she put her had on top of hers.

"That's OK, Peramal. I have been worried about Mama, so I am already emotional. I am so sorry to hear about Ms. Mari," Katherine said with concern in her voice. "Are you doing OK?"

"I am hanging in there. But what is this about your mama? Tell me what's going on."

Katherine went on to explain that her mama had been having really bad headaches, and she was really worried about her. She was planning to take her mother for an MRI and CT scan soon, and she was anxious about the results.

"Can you tell me anything? I know you have this gift, and I hope I am not bothering you by asking you. Is my mama going to be OK?" Katherine's voice trailed off; part of her was afraid of the answer.

Peramal sat quietly and then closed her eyes, trying hard to concentrate on the question. Sometimes she didn't need the water to read because she could feel things. After a few minutes, which seemed like an eternity to Katherine, she finally spoke: "I think your mama is going to be OK. They might find something, but don't be scared. She might have to have surgery, but they can fix the problem. I don't know exactly what it is, but I do know in time she will be OK."

A look of fear came across Katherine's face as she asked, "Does she have a tumor?"

"I don't think so. They will need to do something about it, and she might have to take some medicine. But I think she will be OK." Peramal tried to help her understand. "When is she going for the MRI?"

"She is going next week, on Tuesday."

"I will pray for her that she will be OK."

"Thank you, Peramal. I think that I feel a little better. But I have a confession to make," Katherine said, feeling guilty.

"You don't have to say anything. You came looking for Ms. Mari to find me. Don't worry, it's OK. I already knew, and I am glad you did," Peramal said as she tried to make Katherine feel better.

Katherine smiled and then reached for her purse to give Peramal money.

Peramal looked horrified. "No, please! I don't want your money!" She pushed Katherine's hand back. "I don't take money for this. I only wanted to help you."

Peramal

Katherine looked confused because she remembered hearing from her mother that people paid for a reading.

Peramal went on to explain that it wasn't her, that it was her grandmother that charged the money and forced her to do readings. In her heart she knew it was wrong to make money from her gift—but she was still a child, and she only did it to get her grandmother's approval and, most importantly, her love.

Katherine finally understood, and that realization made her heartache that this wonderful young women had suffered terribly in her life. She still couldn't get the image of when Julio pulled Peramal into the house by the hair at the birthday party all those years ago out of her head. That thought prompted the next question.

"Peramal, I don't mean to pry, but are you still with him?"

Peramal nodded.

"Is he nicer to you?"

"Sometimes, most of the time, I just do my best not to get him angry."

"But why?" Katherine asked, sounding exasperated. "Just leave him!" She has been waiting a long time to have the chance to talk some sense into Peramal, ever since the birthday party.

"I can't!"

"Of course you can!"

"He can be nice; maybe he can change," Peramal tried to convince herself.

"Peramal, please! You have to get away from him!"

"You don't understand! He has threatened to kill me and my kids if I do. I can't let that happen."

"But you can't stay either! We have to figure something out!"

Peramal finally confessed that she been secretly trying to save money, but it had been difficult. If she saved enough, she would buy airplane tickets—although she wasn't sure if she would follow through with it if the time came.

Katherine willingly offered, "Can I buy the tickets for you?"

"That's very generous of you, but I can't accept it. I got myself into this, and I will get myself out of it; that is a promise I made to myself," Peramal spoke vehemently.

"OK, I understand. But when you are ready, you can give me the money, and I will buy the tickets for you, and I will help you get to the airport," Katherine said, hoping that Peramal would agree.

Peramal hadn't thought that far ahead. She was too focused on the money to buy the tickets that she hadn't considered the details of getting there.

"Do you know where you will go?" Katherine asked, as if reading Peramal's mind.

"I want to go to New York."

"Why New York?"

"To find my family. I have an address, but I don't know how to look it up."

"OK, I am going to help you look into that."

"I don't want to bother you."

"You won't bother me! Please let me help you. OK?" Katherine assured her and then offered, "Tell you what, I will come back here in a couple of weeks, and you give me the address. We can stay in touch. I know there is no way that I would be able to call you at home."

"Yes, I really appreciate that. But I want you first to take care of your mama, and then you can help me," Peramal insisted. "But don't worry, she is going to be OK."

"Thank you, Peramal. That makes me feel better," Katherine said as she reached for the bill that the waitress had just placed on the table.

"Oh, no! Please let me pay for lunch!" Peramal said, trying take it away from Katherine.

"Peramal, let me do this, please. This is the least that I can do as a 'thank you' for making me feel better and for praying for my mother." Katherine tried to convince her that it was OK.

The women said their good-byes and went on their way with a promise that they would see other again. In following months, Katherine would frequently stop by, and they would have lunch to talk about their lives. Peramal gave her the New York address, and Katherine promised to do some research.

As Peramal predicted, Katherine's mother, Mrs. González, was diagnosed with an aneurysm that was repaired through surgery; she would have to take medication to prevent seizures and blood clots. But the doctor said that she was OK and could carry on with her life.

From time to time, Peramal would receive postcards and little gifts from Ms. Mari and Dr. Ruiz. They were having a good time, taking it slow in their travels. Ms. Mari would have some good days and some bad days. Every postcard brought a smile to Peramal's face. She collected and saved them in a keepsake box. There was one from postcard from Australia, as well as one from New Zealand. Recently, one had arrived from Huancabamba, Peru, which was in the Andes Mountains and which has many mountain lakes that are home to shaman healers. They would be in South America for a while, the postcard said; perhaps they would be back in Puerto Rico by year's end. Dr. Ruiz's family had a ranch in Santo Domingo, Ecuador, and they might be visiting there as well. There too (also in the Andean region) could be found a group of indigenous healers known as *tsáchila*. Peramal sat quietly, admiring these treasures and dreaming that someday she could travel the world too. With a wistful smile, she put everything back and hid it in the closet next to the box that had her papa's Bible. She had yet to bring herself to go through the letters and Bible that she found at her grandmother's eight years ago. *Someday,* she thought to herself, *someday.*

Before she knew it, it was September and almost a year since Ms. Mari and Dr. Ruiz got married. Victor would be starting fourth grade, and he needed new clothes. It had taken her almost a year to save two hundred dollars, but now she had to use some of it to buy clothes. The clothes that he had couldn't be mended, and the pants were getting too short on him anyway.

"Mama? When are Abuelita and Abuelo coming back? I miss them," Victor asked as he sat watching TV on a quiet Saturday evening, with Melinda soundly in her room.

Peramal looked up from mending some of Julio's socks.

"Hopefully soon, *mijo*. The postcard said probably by the end of this year, which is only three months away." His mother smiled and then went back to the task at hand.

A few minutes later, Julio walked in the room and sat down to put his shoes on. He was going out again. He was never home and didn't spend any time with his children. Peramal felt a wave of fear and anxiety overcome her, and she felt compelled to tell him, "Julio, please don't go; I think something bad is going to happen."

Julio just laughed at her. "You think I am going to fall for that shit. You don't know nothin'. I can't believe people used to pay money for that crap. Bruja!" With that, he turned toward the door to leave, but not before Victor stood up and defended his mother. "Don't say that about mama! Stop being mean to her!"

"Victor! No! Stop!" his mother said as she got up off the couch to stand in front of her son. She got there just as Julio's fist came forward, and he punched her instead of Victor. Peramal fell backward but quickly got up to shield her son again.

"Don't you ever talk that way to me again, boy!" Julio yelled as he knocked over the table lamp, shattering it in a million pieces. Then he stomped out of the house, slamming the door behind him.

"Victor! Are you OK?" Peramal asked her son while she checked his face and arms for any injury.

"I'm fine, Mama! What about you? Your lip is bleeding!"

"It's OK, *mijo*. I will be OK."

"Why do you let him treat you that way? We should just go! He doesn't love us, and he is so mean to you! Please, let's just go!" Victor begged his mother.

"Listen to me. I am working on a way to get us out of here. But, for now, we have to be very careful with how we talk to your father. He is very confused, and he needs help in his head. I am so sorry it has to be this way. You may not believe me, but deep down inside he does love you in his own way."

"It doesn't feel like it."

Peramal looked stunned, she didn't know how to respond to that. She knew her son was right.

At that moment she couldn't keep it together much longer. As she sat down and started to cry, Victor knelt down beside her; tears started rolling down his face. She was getting so tired that she did not have much fight left in her.

It was two-thirty in the morning when the ringing phone woke Peramal up. It was the police. Julio had gotten into a bar fight and was arrested, and she needed to go and bail him out. He had broken a glass bottle over someone's head.

Chapter 12

The next couple of years went by like a blink of an eye. Anytime that she was able to save money to buy airline tickets, something happened, and just like that, the money would disappear.

Katherine was able to locate the address in New York; it belonged to a house that was in Peramal's mother's name. There was a phone number listed as well in the white pages, but when Katherine called it, the "disconnected" message came up. Even though they didn't know a lot about the address, Peramal wanted to go anyway. She desperately wanted to find her mother and explain everything to her about her gift, and that what had happened to her father was not her fault. She really wanted to see her mother, brother, and sister—that was all she could dream about. But she was afraid that they wouldn't remember her; it had been almost twenty years since the last time she saw them. Often she would dream about them and imagine what they would look like now. She remembered that she brought back pictures with her the last time she was at her grandmother's with Ms. Mari.

One Friday evening in October, she decided to pull out the pictures, letters, and her father's Bible. Julio was out again, and she knew he wouldn't be back until the early-morning hours, not unless he was arrested again.

Both Melinda and Victor had fallen asleep, and the house was quiet, with no distractions. Peramal made herself a cup of tea and then sat at the kitchen table. Her heart was racing, and she started to feel very anxious, but she didn't know why.

She looked at the pictures and saw one of her father and mother smiling together on what looked like the day they got married. They were both dressed in nice clothes: her father in a suit and her mother in a simple white dress. Then there were several pictures of Peramal with her brother and sister. She started to imagine how nice it would be when they finally met again; perhaps they could be a family once more. But there was missing a big part, her father. Oh, how she wished that she could see him one more time.

Peramal then turned her attention to a stack of letters and started to read them. It was letters between her mother and grandmother. She couldn't believe what was written. *My mother knew about my gift, and Abuela was giving her money from the readings! This can't be! No! No! No! That's a lie!* Peramal's thoughts started to race as she quickly read through all of the letters, throwing them down to the floor when she was finished.

"They had mastermind the whole thing! My mama never wanted me! She wanted the money!" Peramal said this out loud, as if there was someone else in the room. She was reeling. "But how can this be true? She is my mother!"

A wave of anger and resentment overcame her, and she became hysterical as she picked up the letters and pictures from the floor and started to tear them up into pieces. When she ran out of letters, her hand reached out to grab the Bible that had fallen on to the floor along with the letters. She stopped short and realized that she was about to tear apart her father's Bible. Instead, she held it to her chest as she started to cry, praying for God's help to find peace. Her prayer was answered as a wave a calmness washed over her.

She wiped the tears away from her face and rested on the floor for a second. Then she got up and sat at the table once more. She opened the Bible to read her favorite passage, which she and her father would read together all those years ago.

Then she noticed something strange: there was a section of the Bible that was cut out, and there was a pouch stuffed inside the hole. She opened the pouch to find a wad of money! She couldn't believe what she seeing—there was a small stack of tens and twenties. Peramal counted it up, and it was almost three thousand dollars! She didn't know what to think. *Abuela must have hid it there for safekeeping*, she thought to herself. *This is it! I could use this money to buy the tickets!* Then she started feeling guilty; it wasn't hers to keep.

As she started to clean up the mess, inside she was struggling with herself, trying to convince herself that it would be OK to use the money, and that it was probably her money anyway. She went to bed trying to will herself to sleep, but she kept thinking about the money. She must have fallen asleep eventually, because the next thing she knew, she had woken up to grunting sounds and she felt pain and pressure as Julio was raping her.

Peramal waited for him to finish; she didn't move and she didn't say a word, because if she did, he would beat her up. He was finally done and rolled off of her to his side of the bed and fell asleep.

She quickly got up and went to shower. It was at that moment that she made up her mind and decided to use the money to buy the tickets. She was tired of the abuse from her husband and living in fear, and she needed to see her mother again. Even though the letters clearly showed that her mother was not innocent and she was just as responsible as her grandmother for what had happened to Peramal, she wanted to hear it directly from her. The only way to do that was to go to New York and confront her. Besides, there was nothing left to keep her in San Juan. The last correspondence that she had received from Dr. Ruiz was that Ms. Mari was getting too weak to travel, and he decided that they should stay at his family's ranch in Ecuador for the time being. He also asked that Peramal write him back to let them know if she was doing OK. Peramal sent back a correspondence saying that everything was fine with her and the kids and that Ms. Mari had nothing to worry about. That night, Peramal prayed for God's forgiveness for the lie.

Peramal

Peramal knew she and her children would never be safe while Julio was around. She began planning to give the money to Katherine, so that they might make the trip to New York. She didn't know what they'd find when they got there, but anything was better than this life.

Chapter 13

"Officer Denali? Officer Denali? Are you OK?" Peramal sat across from him in the booth at the diner. He looked stunned, and he didn't know how to respond as she tried to get his attention.

They had been there for almost two hours, during which she had basically told him her life story and why she was homeless at the moment. He couldn't believe all the awful things she'd had to endure.

Earlier, when he had started to drive away, her kids had noticed that she was chasing the police car behind them, and he stopped the car. He took the three of them and bought them breakfast at the diner where he had been with Verde only half an hour before. Now, here he was, sitting across from her, trying to process everything she had told him.

He cleared his throat and finally said, "So this Katherine was able to get you the tickets and take you to the airport. How were you able to get away from him?" Edward couldn't bring himself to say Julio's name. No woman should ever be treated that way, and this animal made him sick to his stomach.

Peramal

Peramal continued with her story. "It wasn't easy. He was usually drunk or wasted most of the time and never paid any attention. But for some reason, he became suspicious that day," she explained. "I made an excuse that I had to go to work on a Saturday, so I had the kids with me. He never took care of them, and I never let him. But that day, he decided to follow me."

Once Katherine bought the tickets, Peramal had slowly started to take some clothes and necessities, such as birth certificates and other important documents, to work and left them there. She explained everything to Mr. Santiago. Although he was sad to see her go, he understood.

When the day finally came, Katherine was waiting there at the dress shop. Soon after, Peramal showed up with the kids, and Julio was right behind them. He attacked Peramal and tried to choke her right in front of her kids. Mr. Santiago was able to overpower him because Julio was still intoxicated. Peramal got away from him, and then she tried to apologize and told him he needed help. Julio just responded by spitting at her; he called her every name in book and threatened to kill her.

Peramal turned away and never looked back. They quickly piled into Katherine's car and took off. A police car showed up a minute later and took Julio into custody, where he spent the night in jail.

On the way to the airport, Peramal put the whole ordeal out of her mind and focused on what was happening next. Katherine handed her an envelope with the tickets and other important information. She explained to Peramal that there was a hotel near the address they had for her mother's house, in case Peramal needed a place to stay temporarily. Katherine also gave Peramal paid phone cards that Peramal could use to call her from any payphone in case she needed her help. There was still plenty of money left to get Peramal by until she was situated and hopefully reunited with her mother and siblings.

When Peramal and her kids got to New York, they took a taxi to the address that was on the envelope that she had held on to for twenty years. The house was old and beat up. A man answered the door, and she recognized him as her brother, A. J. He wasn't very welcoming, but he seemed very surprised to see her. He was now married and had two sons a little older than Victor. From the looks of them, they were not that friendly either. She got the feeling they were members of a gang.

Peramal was disappointed to find out that her mother wasn't there. She had moved down to Florida with Peramal's sister, Sophia. Since it was late, Peramal asked if they could stay the night, and in the morning they would find a place to stay. At first, A. J. refused, but then happily agreed when Peramal offered to give him some money. Then he told her that she could stay as long as she wanted, as long as she paid him. Neither one of his sons would give up their rooms, so they had to make do with the garage.

It was the second night there that one of the sons snuck into the garage and stole whatever money she had left, as well as the phone cards. They were now penniless. She tried to tell her brother that the money was stolen, but he didn't believe her and threatened to throw her and her kids out in the street.

Peramal promised that she would go out and find a job. However, this proved to be next to impossible. She had to walk everywhere she went, and took the kids along with her. She knew it wasn't safe to leave them behind at her brother's house. Her nephew's friend hung out there, and sometimes she would find him looking at her daughter.

Peramal simply couldn't find a job. She couldn't blame them—who was going to hire someone who was homeless and had her kids in tow? A week went by and still no luck.

Her brother confronted her. "Where is my money?"

"I'm sorry, A. J.," Peramal cried. "Please give me some more time!"

"You could make money! You are a *bruja*! Just read the water, and you can make a lot of it—or maybe you could live with Cousin Alberto!" he said with a smirk on his face. Then he threatened, "We are going out, and I better find you and your kids gone by the time we get back. If you are not, I will throw you out myself!"

Melinda and Victor were cowering in the corner of the garage when she went there to get them and gather their stuff so they could leave. The sound of the argument frightened them.

"*Mis amores*, don't be scared. It's going to be OK." Peramal tried to coax her children out of the corner.

"Are we going to Cousin Alberto's?" Melinda innocently asked.

Peramal cringed inwardly but agreed because she did not know what else to say.

"Let's go get some food from the kitchen," she instructed her children. She didn't feel bad about taking the food because her nephews had stolen her money.

Peramal found a bag and put the food items in it. As she turned to walk out, she noticed a postcard from Florida stuck to the refrigerator. It was from her mother, and there was an address. She quickly got a piece of paper and copied the information.

Then they left her brother's house. They did find a shelter, but it was going to be dangerous there. That's how they ended up on the park bench, where Edward had found them.

❧

Once again, the police officer looked stunned. Her story sounded like a soap opera that his wife, Cecelia, liked to watch. Cecelia practically watched every single soap opera there was on TV and didn't spend much time doing anything else besides shopping or getting her nails done.

"What are you going to do now?" Edward asked.

It took that question to make her realize that she had no idea what would become of her or her kids, and that thought broke heart. She didn't care what happened to her; all she cared about was the safety and well-being of her children.

"I don't know," she whispered softly before she broke down and started to cry as she covered her face with her hands. Her children looked worried.

Edward tried to console her.

"Look, I am going to make some calls. I think there is a shelter on the East Side, which is in the better part of town. OK?" Denali tried to make her feel better.

Peramal removed her hands from her face and tried to smile when she thanked him. Then she asked, "Why do you want to help me? Why are you being so nice to me?"

Edward was silent for a minute and then replied, "Honestly, I'm not sure. I just know that you're a good person stuck in a bad situation."

Then he remembered to tell her about the lottery win. He smiled when he said, "Or maybe because you brought me luck! I took your advice and won a hundred dollars!" He reached in his wallet to give her money. "I think you deserve some of it."

Peramal looked embarrassed and turned it down. "No, please, I don't want it. It's your money and not mine. But I do want to tell you: you should keep playing from time to time. One day you are going to win big!"

"OK." He smiled and agreed. "Why don't you take the kids and wait in that abandoned warehouse while I make some calls?"

True to his word, he came back for them and drove them to the women's shelter.

On the drive over, Edward wanted to make conversation, so he asked, "Are you going to try and find your mother? Didn't you say that you found an address for her?"

"Yes, I did. I feel like I am on a wild goose chase, but I am going have to try. I need to face her. I need to know the truth about the letters and whether she purposely left me behind." Her voice sounded very sad and angry at the same time.

He didn't know what else to say to make her feel better. Instead he suggested, "Take it one day at a time. Let's get you situated so that you have a place to stay, and we can find you a job and get the kids in school. I will also put you in touch with the social worker that works with the police department. Don't worry, it will all be OK." He smiled at her and then turned his attention back to the road. Neither of them spoke again for the rest of the car ride, and the kids fell asleep.

When they arrived, Peramal noticed that the place seemed very nice and clean, and the staff was very kind. They were all women, and she was relieved that wouldn't have to deal with any unwanted advances. A month went by, and Peramal started to feel anxious; she wanted to find a place with more privacy than the shelter. But she had to wait until the social worker that Edward mentioned was available to stop by. She would be able to help Peramal find something a little more permanent.

They spent another month in the shelter, but eventually, Peramal and her kids were set up in community housing. It was not the best of circumstances because they had to share a house with three other mothers with their children, but at least she had privacy and some semblance of normalcy. The other mothers mostly kept to themselves; each of them had her own horrible story of violence and abuse. Melinda and Victor were enrolled in the schools nearby. Since Peramal was a seamstress, the social worker was able to help her find a job at a clothing factory. Because of her prior work experience, she was able to make a decent amount of money.

Every now and then, Officer Denali would stop by, and they would have coffee. It was so nice talking with him, like they had known each other for years. It had already been six months since they met in October. Spring was just around the corner, and the weather was beautiful in New York, but she still missed this time of the year in Puerto Rico. Sometimes she would get homesick, but she would put those thoughts out of her mind because she didn't want to think about Julio. She had no idea how she was going deal with that situation. All she knew was that eventually she wanted to divorce him.

It was a beautiful Saturday morning, and Peramal took her kids to play in the nearby park. They were adjusting well to the school, but they wanted a place of their own. Peramal was doing her best to save money, but for now they had to make do. In the back of her mind, she already had made plans that when the time was right, she would go to Florida to find her mother. But part of her didn't want to go; she really enjoyed seeing Edward and talking with him. It didn't hurt that he was so handsome, though not in the classic sense. He had beautiful blue eyes, dark-blond hair, and very rugged features; she guessed he was in his late thirties. He had a slender build and was tall, probably four inches taller than her, but nowhere near the height of Dr. Ruiz, who was over six feet.

She wondered what it would be like to kiss him, but she quickly put that thought out of her mind. He was married, and she was content being his friend.

"Hey, stranger." Peramal was startled by a voice behind her. It was Officer Denali.

She started to blush, but luckily, he didn't notice as he came over and sat next to her on the park bench. "We've got to stop meeting like this," he said with a smile, referring to the first time they met, when he saw her on a park bench and then kicked her off.

"Hola, Edward. Good to see you. It has been a while."

He had not been around in about a month. He had been taking extra shifts to earn extra money. His wife had just found out she was pregnant, and so he wanted to start saving money. Peramal was happy to hear the wonderful news, but she was sad at the same time—she was afraid for the baby. In her heart, she prayed that God blessed the pregnancy.

Peramal wished him well. "Congratulations on the baby. I am so happy for you. You will make a good father." She meant that from the bottom of her heart.

"I hope so." Edward replied, with a smile, and then turned his attention to Melinda and Victor, who were at the swings. "Your kids look like they are doing great."

"Yes, they are. Thank God," Peramal said. "I know this is still hard on them, and I am doing the best I can."

"Yes, you are! Don't ever doubt that!" Officer Denali agreed wholeheartedly.

"Why did you become a police officer?" Peramal asked out of the blue, and then she realized that she had taken him by surprise. "I am sorry. I shouldn't have asked that."

"Oh no. That's OK," he replied. "I guess because it's in my family. My father was, and his father was. I also have a cousin and uncle that are now. I guess you could say it's in my blood. Who knows? Maybe my son or daughter will become a police officer one day!" He paused for a second and then said, "Why do you ask?"

"Well, if I tell you, you promise not to laugh." Peramal smiled shyly.

"Cross my heart." Denali made the sign of the cross on his chest and promised.

"I have always thought about being one, or maybe working as a detective or something like this. I like to solve mysteries," she finally confessed.

"I think that is great! You should go for it! Especially if you have that psychic ability; it would be phenomenal!" the officer encouraged her. She once shared that dream of becoming a police officer with Julio, and he had just laughed in her face and made fun of her. It was so nice to have someone finally believe in her, besides Ms. Mari.

He then asked, "Do you have your high school diploma?" With that, her excitement quickly deflated, and it appeared evident on her face.

"No. I don't." She admitted, and put her head down.

"Hey. That's OK," he said encouragingly. "You can get your GED. Maybe we can check at Victor's school; they have a high school there, and it is within walking distance of the community housing." Then another realization came to him.

He felt bad for asking, but he knew he had to. "Do you know how to drive?"

Peramal shook her head.

"Then we can work on that too. Well, I have got to get going, but I will stop by in a few days so we can get the ball rolling," he said as he waved good-bye. Then he went to his squad car and drove away.

His wife is very lucky to have him, Peramal thought as she called the kids over so they could get back to the house and get some dinner. That night she had a wonderful dream about being happy and content; she was living in a big mansion. She knew that would never happen, but it was still nice to dream.

The next few months went by so quickly. Peramal learned to drive and got her GED. She couldn't believe all of the wonderful things that were happening to her, and it was all thanks to Edward.

His wife had a baby boy, and he was on cloud nine. They named him Joseph, after his father. But not too long after the baby was born, they discovered that he needed heart surgery, and Denali was devastated. But Peramal tried to assure him that his son was going to be OK.

Everything did go well with the surgery, but Denali's son needed extra attention and care for the first year of his life. After that, he would be able to live a normal life. His wife wanted to move closer to her mother in Rochester—a seven-hour drive—to get help with the baby. Denali had to put in for a transfer, which meant he wouldn't be able to see Peramal again. He had come to really enjoy their friendship and long talks—they had so much in common even though they came from different walks of life. He was going to miss her terribly.

The day had come for Denali to say good-bye. Peramal was devastated, and she couldn't stop crying that day. She treasured his friendship, and she felt like they were soul mates. She didn't want it to end, but she knew he was doing the right thing. She wasn't sure if they would ever see each other again—perhaps in another lifetime.

"Well, I guess this is it." Peramal spoke first, trying to be brave. "Thank you for all that you did for us and for believing in me."

"You don't have to thank me. You are a good person. You did this all by yourself." Edward felt very emotional. He reached out to give her a hug, and part of him didn't want to let her go. In the last few months that they had known each other, this was the first time they had ever hugged, it felt nice and familiar. It took great strength for Denali to let her go—it got too dangerous too fast.

To keep the moment from ending, because he wasn't ready to say good-bye yet, he started to make small talk.

"Are you still planning to go to Florida to find your mother?"

"Yes, eventually. I want to save some money, buy a car, and drive down there."

Edward nodded and said, "I hope you find her. Whatever happened to Ms. Mari and her husband?"

"Part of me is afraid to write to find out because I don't want to hear bad news. I am better off not knowing."

"Do you feel something? I mean, I don't how this stuff works…do think you she is OK? Wasn't she seeing some shaman healers?"

"I am not sure. I have tried to block it out of my mind; I am trying not to feel anything. I haven't dreamed about her in a long time. I am not sure what that means."

They stared quietly at each other, and Edward fidgeted with his police hat. It seemed like an eternity before he finally spoke again, his voice heavy with emotion. "I better go. It's getting late."

"Don't forget to play the lottery," Peramal said, trying to be light-hearted. But that was tough, since she was trying to hold back tears.

He smiled that sweet smile of his and got into his squad car, and just like that, he was out of her life.

Chapter 14

"Are we there yet?" Melinda asked probably for the hundredth time since they had left New York six hours earlier. Seven-year-olds can be so impatient.

"Not yet, *mija*," her mother replied in tired a voice. "We will still have about sixteen more hours of driving, but we will probably need to stop for gas, food, and to get some rest, so it will take a little longer. But, don't worry, we will get there." She tried to smile and show the kids that this was a wonderful adventure.

Peramal had managed to save about six thousand dollars during her time in New York. In August 2001, she left for Florida, almost a year to the day that she had to say good-bye to Edward. Oh, how she missed him and hoped that he was happy. She was able to buy a used car for about two thousand dollars, and had the rest came in handy to cover their expenses for the move.

They finally made it to Clearwater, Florida. With the various stops, it took close to two days. It was almost eight o'clock in the evening, and the sun was still shining, bright and very humid. Although that would seem uncomfortable to anyone else, for Peramal it almost felt like being home in Puerto Rico.

She followed the driving directions that she had printed out at the library in New York. The address took her to a trailer park. Since it was almost nine o'clock at night, she did not want to barge in on her mother and sister this late. It had been almost twenty years since she saw them last, so another few hours wasn't going to make a difference. As luck would have it, there was a motel around the corner, and there were vacancies. They got a room for the night to shower and get some rest.

As she was tucking in Melinda, she made them both a promise that if they liked it in Florida that they would stay there and make a life for themselves. She wanted to give them stability and a place to call their own. They both mumbled their I love yous and good-nights and promptly fell asleep.

Finally, it was morning, and Peramal hadn't gotten a wink of sleep. Her stomach was in knots. She wasn't sure if she could blame the lack of sleep on being in a strange room or on the idea that soon she would be able to confront her mother. She probably managed to sleep for a few minutes before she found herself dreaming that she was driving toward a cement wall and the brakes weren't working, so she couldn't stop the car. It was going faster and faster, and just before she was going to crash, she woke up screaming and found herself in the motel room. Her kids were still sound asleep.

It was finally time to get up. She helped Melinda get ready while Victor got himself ready. They piled into the car, and

Peramal

Peramal went to a fast-food drive-through and got breakfast for her kids and just coffee for herself since she was too nervous to eat.

About an hour later, Peramal finally got the nerve to go see her mother. They arrived at the trailer park and found the address number. She felt dizzy as she got out of the car; her heart started to race, and her mouth was so dry that it was hard for her to speak. It took a moment to steady herself. "This is it," she mumbled to herself.

"OK, my loves, come on out, and stay close to me," she instructed her children. Victor got out first and went around to get his sister.

Peramal climbed the two short steps and knocked on the door. She braced herself for what was to come next. But nothing came; there was no answer. Then she tried again, knocking a little louder the second time.

"If you are looking for Iris Otero, she is long gone," said a male voice from behind them. "I'm Charlie, the manager; how can I help you?"

It took a second as Peramal tried to swallow and take a breath before she was able to speak.

"I'm her daughter. Do you know where she might be? Is she coming back?" Peramal asked, her voice shaky. It felt like she was being abandoned all over again, like that day in the kitchen with her grandmother all those years ago.

"I don't think so. She moved out a couple of months ago and didn't leave a forwarding address. I'm sorry. If you need anything else, I'm in the office at the entrance of the trailer park. Have a nice day," said the manager as he continued on his way.

Peramal mumbled a thank you and got her children in the car. She drove to the local supermarket and picked up some water, milk, and few other basic items. They returned to the motel, and she paid for a week's stay. They settled in. She pushed small coffee table to provide extra security for the door.

She told the kids that they could watch TV and that she needed a nap. All she wanted to do was sleep and forget her worries, at least for the next few hours.

※

It was late January 2002, and Mckenna had finally settled into a routine in her new life in Florida. She had gotten married just that past December, and she and her husband, James, had gone to Australia, where her husband was from. He wanted his wife to meet his family. After the honeymoon, they had returned to Portland, Oregon, where Mckenna was from, to pack up and ship her things to her new home in Clearwater. Her new husband was an attorney based there. When James and Mckenna decided to get married, they agreed that Mckenna would have to move, since James had his law practice well established. Mckenna was a children's book author, so she was could work from anywhere. She published her first book through an independent publishing platform. By sheer luck, it was noticed by a rather large publishing house, and they made her an offer to publish her second book. This experience had been rather exciting but stressful at the same time because she had recently found out that she was pregnant. The couple was very excited, but they couldn't believe how quickly it happened, especially because Mckenna was in her late thirties.

Because both writing the book and taking care of the house would be too difficult, James convinced his wife that they needed someone to help take care of the house. He hired a service to come clean once a week.

"Sweetheart, don't forget that the cleaning people are coming tomorrow," James reminded his wife as they sat down to dinner.

"I truly appreciate it, but I think I can manage myself. It is just strange for me; I'm not used to someone taking care of my things."

"Trust me, it will be great, and you can spend more time— especially now that you are resting and eating for two!" James said jokingly.

"Hey! Watch it, mister!" Mckenna laughingly warned her husband as he moved over to give his wife a soft kiss on the lips.

The next morning, Mckenna ran around the house organizing and frantically putting things away.

"Love?" James spoke in his thick Australian accent, "What are you doing? You shouldn't be moving or carrying heavy things. That is why I got you the help."

"I know, but it is easier to clean when things are not so cluttered."

"OK, but please don't do too much. I should be home by six," James said as he drank the last sip of coffee and kissed his wife and left for work.

"Love you. Have a great day."

Mckenna made herself some decaf coffee, grabbed a banana, and then walked over to her home office. The morning sickness had not set in yet, but it but she was feeling tired and sometimes a bit cranky. She sat at her desk, adjusted her computer, and started to type away. She got so engrossed in her writing that an hour had gone by when she was startled by the sound of the doorbell. For a second, she forgot who it could be; then she remembered it was the cleaning service.

She opened the door to find a young woman carrying a vacuum and cleaning supplies.

"Hello, I am looking for Mrs. Prescott. I'm Peramal. I am here to do the cleaning."

"Yes. Hi. Come on in. I'm Mckenna Prescott."

"Hello. Nice to meet you. Your house is beautiful."

"Thank you." Mckenna smiled and showed Peramal around.

"Let me know if you need anything, Peramal. That is a beautiful name by the way. Did I pronounce correctly?"

"Yes, perfect. I will get started."

"OK. Can I get you some coffee or water?"

"I'm OK now. Maybe some water a little later. Thank you."

"No worries. I will be in my office down the hall if you need anything. Also, you don't have to worry about cleaning my office every time. I might have it done just every once in a while," Mckenna said as she walked back to her office.

Peramal made her way to the master bedroom to get started. She put her headset on and focused on the tasks at hand for the next couple of hours. Peramal noticed that the house was clean and well organized. She was happy about that; it made her life easier. She was also glad that there were no cats. Although she had nothing against cats, she was allergic to them to a point that it was sometimes hard for her to breathe around them. The first time she was sent to a house with cats, she ended up going to urgent care, where she was prescribed an inhaler with steroids to control the asthma attack. Peramal did not realize that she had asthma until she started this job. This was a temporary situation, though. She had recently enrolled in technical college to get her degree so she could perhaps apply for the police academy or work at a police station or courthouse.

Peramal was thirsty and wanted to ask for the water. She walked back to Mrs. Prescott's office and knocked on the door, which was slightly ajar.

"Come in."

"Sorry to bother you, but may I have some water?"

"Sure, go ahead and grab it from the refrigerator."

Peramal noticed that Mckenna was not looking good. She was pale white and had a terrified look on her face. Although Peramal just met her, she felt like that she was a nice person and wanted to ask if she needed anything.

"Excuse me, Mrs. Prescott, but are you OK? Can I do something for you?"

Mckenna was going to lie and tell her she was fine, but she was scared and needed someone to talk to. "Actually, I'm not doing so good."

"What can I do? Do you want me to call someone?" Peramal asked with concern in her voice.

"I am not sure if anyone can help. I'm about six weeks pregnant, and I started to bleed. I called the doctor, but they said they may not be able to help me. But they are going to see me anyway to do an ultrasound."

"I am so sorry. But I think you are going to be OK. Sometimes these things happen. Don't worry." Peramal was not sure why she even said that, but something made her.

"Thank you for your kind words," Mckenna replied, but she was still was not convinced that it would be OK.

"I am actually almost done. Do you need me to help you to the car, so you could go to the doctor?" Peramal offered.

"I will be fine. I need to leave in about an hour."

Peramal turned around to walk out of the room, when she felt like she to say one more thing.

"I know this sounds crazy and you are not going to believe me, but I really think you will be fine, and you are going to find out that you are having twins."

Mckenna was floored and was not sure how to respond to that. She asked, "Why do you think that I am having twins?"

"Well, when I was cleaning your house, I saw that you had two lizards, each in a different room." When she said it out loud, she realized how crazy it sounded and wished that she didn't say anything.

Mckenna was skeptical but fascinated at the same time. If she wasn't scared out of her mind at the moment, she would have wanted to know more and asked questions. She had always been interested in the whole area of psychic phenomena.

Before Mckenna had a chance to say anything, she noticed that Peramal blushed with embarrassment as she apologized if she had said anything out of turn; then, she quickly ran out of the room.

❈

It was the longest twenty-minute wait for the doctor to come in and do the ultrasound. Mckenna sat on the cold examination table, silently praying and thinking about what Peramal had said. Mckenna was thirty-six, and her grandmother on her father's side did have two sets of twins. Both of those factors can contribute to the likelihood of twins. The thought of twins had never really crossed her mind until now. *How incredible would that be, and how would James feel about that?* she thought. But then she realized that she shouldn't get ahead of herself. Her thoughts were interrupted by the doctor knocking on the door and then coming in.

They exchanged pleasantries, and then he got to work and started to conduct the ultrasound. It felt cold and gooey when he inserted the device. Mckenna held her breath, waiting for him to say something. *Oh, please, God, let everything be OK!* she thought.

"Everything seems to look good; no sign of a miscarriage," Dr. Roy gave her the good news. "It must be an irritation of the cervix."

"Thank God," Mckenna whispered as a wave of relief washed over her. Then she had to ask, "Dr. Roy, what are the chances of my having twins? Twins do run in my family."

"Funny you should ask, I just noticed what looked like two flicker spots which would be the hearts beating. I'd say there might be a chance that you are carrying twins, but we won't know for sure until a few weeks from now."

Mckenna only half listened to what else he was saying. *Could Peramal be right?* she thought.

The doctor finished the ultrasound and told her to make an appointment in the next couple of weeks, just to make sure things were progressing well.

On her way home, she decided to call James; she couldn't wait for him to come home to tell him. On the first ring, he answered his cell.

"Hello, darling," Mckenna said.

"Hello, love."

"Are you sitting down?"

"What's wrong? You are scaring me! Is it the baby?"

Mckenna went on to explain about the bleeding and that thank goodness everything was fine. James was upset that she hadn't called him earlier, because he wanted to be there for her.

"Sweetheart, I'm OK. I knew that you had several meetings, and I wanted to be sure what was going on before I got you worried too."

"So why did I have to be sitting down?"

"Well, he is not a hundred percent sure now, but there is a possibility that it might be twins." Mckenna waited for James to say something, but there was silence.

"James? Are you there?" It took a few seconds, but he finally responded.

"Yes, I'm here. Wow! Twins! That is incredible!"

"Are you happy about that?"

"Of course, love, I was just getting over the initial shock! Twins! How cool is that! Oh, I love you so much!"

"I love you too. See you later." Mckenna hung up the phone and smiled happily while she thanked God for this blessing. She wanted to tell James about what Peramal said, but she thought it would be too much for him to handle right now—definitely another day.

❦

After finishing the Prescott house, Peramal had two other jobs to finish before going to pick up her kids from summer camp at their school.

It had been ten months since that day she moved down to Florida from New York. She had put aside her the idea of finding her mother and focused on her life moving forward. She found an apartment and a job cleaning houses. The kids were enrolled in school, trying to get on with their lives. Victor was almost fourteen and ready to get his driver's permit the following year. He was graduating from middle school soon and he was doing really well. Oftentimes, he would talk about going to college, and that made Peramal really happy. In a couple years, he would need a car, and she started to save a little money when she could. By then, he could get a job so he could pay his way through college. About six months ago, Peramal had decided that she wanted to do more for herself, so she looked into the local technical school. She was able to get some financial help, and she enrolled. She started taking courses once a week, on her day off.

The week quickly went by, and it was time to go back to the Prescott house. She was actually surprised that they wanted her back. Peramal thought for sure that they would have called her boss and asked for another of his employees.

She knocked on the door, and it immediately swung open. Mckenna welcomed her in and reached out to give her a hug that took Peramal by surprise.

"Peramal, I am so happy to see you!"

"Hello, Mrs. Prescott. It is nice to see you too. Are you feeling better?"

"Please call me Mckenna, and, yes, I am more than OK! You were right about everything!"

"I'm so glad to hear that; you made my day."

"Come sit down. Can I get you some coffee?" Mckenna offered.

"Sure. I take it black with two sugars. Thank you."

The two women sat together, and Mckenna shared the good news about what Peramal had already predicted. Peramal went on to tell her about her gift. Over the following months, they became fast friends; they were soon as close as sisters.

Sometimes Peramal would read for Mckenna, and they would talk about their lives. It was hard for Mckenna to hear some of things that her friend had gone through. She did enjoy hearing about Edward and was glad someone was there to help her during her time in New York. They developed a bond of friendship that they both treasured.

The months flew by, and it was time. Mckenna gave birth to twins, healthy baby girls, and they named them Georgia and Nicole—after George and Nicholas, their grandfathers. One of girls looked like her father, and the other like her mother, just as Peramal had predicted.

Chapter 15

"All rise for the Honorable Judge Salvador Rodríguez," the bailiff ordered the occupants of the courtroom. Julio sat behind the screened-off section of the courtroom that was designated for the inmates. He was wearing a prison jumpsuit with numbers written across the chest. He looked dazed, disoriented, and extremely thin. His lawyer, a public defender, sat on a bench on the other side. It was finally Julio's turn, and then it was all over in five minutes—an open-and-shut case of involuntary manslaughter. There were multiple witnesses in the bar who had seen Julio strike the victim in the head with an empty beer bottle. But that was not the cause of death; it happened when the victim fell backward, hitting his head against the edge of the table, and then it was all over—he couldn't be saved. Julio was sentenced to ten years in prison and could be eligible for parole in eight years, with good behavior. Due to the fact he was a repeat offender, the judge was hard on him. Most of the previous charges against Julio were mainly domestic violence and assault, and now he accidently took a life.

It had been a little over two years since he last saw Peramal that day in the dress shop. In some moments of clarity, he realized how awful he had been to her, and he couldn't blame her for leaving him. But then the angry side of him took over, and his desire to kill her was stronger than ever. If he had the money, he probably would have gone after her, but he had nothing. He was able to track down his father and moved in with him. Juan had remarried, and his stepmother was not too pleased to have Julio around, which led to the various altercations and his short stints in prison. But this time he was going to get put away for a long time. At that point, he didn't care. He was just waiting for the day Peramal would come back. They were still married, and that was something he was going to hang on to and hold over her.

It would be a day or two before he would be transported to the maximum-security prison. A guard came by to get him. "Hey, Collazo, you got a visitor."

"Who is it?" Julio was excited because he assumed it was Peramal. He knew she would come crawling back to him, asking for his forgiveness. Well, he would show her forgiveness the next time he could get his hands on her.

"The queen," the guard said sarcastically. "Just get up and go there and find out for yourself."

Julio got up and walked ahead of the guard. There was an air of arrogance about him, like he was king of the world. As Julio turned the corner, his eyes scanned all of the visitors behind the glass looking for Peramal, but he couldn't find her. The guard pushed him along, to the chair at the far end of the room, their shoes squeaking on the linoleum floor the whole way. He wasn't able to see who it was because of the dividers. When he got to the chair, he looked to see that it was not Peramal, but rather his aunt Mari with her husband, Eric. He became very angry and just wanted to lash out. He picked up the receiver and said, "It's you. I thought you would be dead by now."

Ms. Mari was taken aback by his greeting, like she had been punched in the stomach. Eric tried to take the phone from her because he wanted to put Julio in his place. From Mari's reaction, he knew Julio probably said something insulting. Mari mumbled that she was OK because she didn't want to cause a scene.

"How are you, Julio?"

"How do you think I am, and how did you know I was here?"

"When we got back into to town, we didn't find you, Peramal, or the kids. So we got worried. Eric made some calls and found out you were here."

At the sound of Peramal's name, Julio became very angry and started cussing.

"You better tell that bitch that she is still my wife and she better come and see me!"

Mari was horrified and wondered how someone could be so cruel. "Watch your language! Why do you have to be so mean all the time? That girl has been through so much with you, and all she ever did was try to make you happy. But that was never enough for you!"

Mari had always wanted to say these things to him, but she was always afraid of him. But, now with the thick glass separating them, she felt safe enough to tell him how she really felt.

"I did nothin'! She got what she deserved!"

Mari ignored his response and pushed him to find out where Peramal could have gone.

"Do you know where Peramal went?" She held her breath, hoping that he would tell her. Part of her was afraid that he had killed her and the kids and buried them somewhere. But the fact that he was so agitated upon hearing Peramal's name made her feel better, because obviously, he honestly had no idea where she had gone.

"I don't know where that whore went!"

"Where was the last time you saw her? Who was she with? Just tell me something!"

Julio thought for a second as he tried to remember, and then he did, but he was not about to reveal that information to his aunt. He was hoping that his father would be able to help him to track her down, and he was not going to let Mari have a head start.

"I don't remember," he said with a smirk on his face. "I guess you will never find her."

He then hung up the receiver, stood up, and was led away by the guard.

Eric put his hands on his wife's shoulders to comfort her as she started to cry.

"Come, my love. Let's go. We will find her, don't worry."

"Oh, Eric, I am so afraid we will never see her again."

Mari stood up from the chair, feeling tired from jet lag as she leaned toward her husband for support. Eric put his arm around her waist, and they walked out of the jail.

Eric and Mari had arrived from Ecuador the night before. They were getting worried that Peramal had not been answering their letters or phone calls and flew back to Puerto Rico. By some miracle, the time she had spent with the shaman healers had improved Mari's strength and well-being. She had started feeling like her old self again, and perhaps she was even healed. Eric had suggested that they do some new scans to see if there was any improvement, but Mari didn't want to. If God had decided to give her a second chance, then she would take it, with no questions asked, and she didn't need a test to tell her that.

On the drive home, Mari was quiet and lost in thought. She tried to rack her brain about where Peramal could have gone. Then it dawned on her where they could start: Mr. Santiago's dress shop.

"*Mi amor*, if you are not too tired, could we go to Mr. Santiago's? Maybe he will know," Mari asked her husband, feeling hopeful.

"Of course, my love, anything for you," Eric said as he leaned over to give his wife a kiss on the lips.

They arrived at the dress shop, only to find that Mr. Santiago was no longer there. He had sold the shop and then decided to retire and move to West Palm Beach, to live with his son and daughter-in-law.

"I'm sorry, Mari. I wish I could help you. I'm not sure how to get a hold of him," said Ivette, one of the seamstresses whom Mari used to work with a long time ago. Ivette had come back to the store and was now its owner.

"That's OK. How long ago did he leave?"

"A while ago—maybe two years now. He was having a hard time with this man that kept coming around destroying the store and the merchandise. The stress took a toll on Mr. Santiago, and so he decided to retire. For whatever reason, this man was blaming Mr. Santiago for his wife leaving him. Last I heard, this man was in jail now, serving time for killing someone."

Mari and Eric looked at each other because they both knew that she was talking about Julio.

"Do you know what happened to the wife and where she might have gone? Did she have kids with her?"

Ivette seemed oblivious to the specific questions she was being asked and didn't ask why they wanted to know. She just wanted to be nice and help her old coworker. "Well, from how I remember Mr. Santiago telling the story, the wife had come to the store with her kids, and this other woman was there to take her and her kids to the airport. But the husband followed them and tried to choke his wife."

Mari started reeling and was afraid that her worst nightmare had come true. She turned ghost-white and turned to Eric, looking for support. Eric move closer to her and grabbed his wife's hand. His heart started to race, as he too feared the worst.

Before Mari was able to get the words out, Eric spoke first, his voice fraught with emotion. "The wife? Was she OK? Did he....? I mean is she...?" His voice trailed off because he couldn't bring himself to say those words.

Ivette started to look confused; she couldn't figure out why they both reacted as they did, but she quickly wanted to assure them that the wife was OK.

"From what Mr. Santiago told me, the wife was fine. He was able to pull the husband off of her, and then she, with her two kids and this other woman, got into a car, and they were able to get away."

The older couple was visibly shaken and relieved at the same time. At least they knew that Peramal had gotten away, but where did she go?

"Did Mr. Santiago tell you who the woman that took them away in the car was? Do you by chance know her name?" Mari asked.

"No, I don't remember if he ever did. I'm sorry," Ivette said as she turned to find a waiting customer. "If you would excuse me, I need to take care of this customer. Leave me your number; if I remember anything else, I can give you a call."

Eric and Mari left the shop and got into their car.

"Who do you suppose this woman was?" Eric asked his wife. "In the short time that I knew her, it didn't seem like she had any friends."

Mari was lost in thought, trying to figure out who it might be.

"You're right, *mi amor*. She didn't have any because Julio wouldn't let her..." Her voice trailed off because she started to remember something, and then it was like a light bulb suddenly went on in her head. "I've got it! I bet it was Katherine!"

"Who's Katherine?"

Peramal

"Katherine's mother was Peramal's grandmother's neighbor. How they met is a long story, but Katherine lives here in town, and for a time Peramal and Katherine were becoming good friends until Julio put a stop to it. Let's go home; I should have her number there!" Mari was excited because she felt like she was one step closer to tracking down Peramal.

They made it home, and Mari raced to her address book to look for the number.

"Got it!" She was turning to grab the house phone when Eric came up to her.

"Mari, *mi amor*, slow down. Take a deep breath. You need to take it easy," he said as he took the receiver from her hand.

"OK! OK! I am calm," she said as she took a couple of breaths, inhaling and exhaling. "There, I'm done. Now please give me the phone."

"Oh Mari! What am I going to do with you!" Eric said laughingly. His wife smiled up at him and gave him a peck on the cheek before turning to make the call.

She was relieved when Katherine answered the phone. They exchanged pleasantries, and then Mari had asked about Peramal. Katherine sounded distraught as she explained what had happened, and that she never had heard from Peramal in almost two years. Katherine had even tried to contact the police and hospitals in New York, but no one ever heard of that name. In a way, though, she thought this was a good thing, because it meant that Peramal was doing OK—or at least Katherine hoped she was. She had even tried to send letters to that New York address, but the letters came back marked "return to sender."

Mari asked for that New York address and thanked Katherine for trying to help Peramal. Katherine made Mari promise her she would keep her posted when she found Peramal.

When she hung up the phone, Mari turned to her husband and said, "We have to go to New York."

"But Mari, you can't go to New York. You are just regaining your strength. I am not going to let you risk your health."

"Please, Eric, we have to find her. I need to know that she and the kids are OK!"

"I will hire a detective. We will find them. *¿Sí?*"

Mari wanted to argue with him and insist on going, but she knew he was right.

"You're right," Mari softly whispered as she reached over to hug her husband.

After two weeks on the job, the detective turned up nothing. There was no trace of Peramal anywhere. The detective needed more information on Peramal, so he stopped by Eric and Mari's home one evening in late April.

"She couldn't have just disappeared into thin air, Mr. Torres." Mari sounded frustrated, but she was trying hard not to take it out on the detective.

"Please call me Xavier. I have tried everything. I went to the address in New York, and her brother wasn't very helpful. He wouldn't tell me anything."

The detective then pulled out his notebook to look at the information that he had. "Her name is quite unusual, so

I thought it would be easier to track her down. Maybe I did not get the correct spelling? I have it as P-e-r-a-m-a-l, and her maiden name is Otero, and her married name is Collazo. The date of birth is June 8, 1971. Right?"

"No! No! No!" Mari exclaimed. "I can't believe that I forgot this! Her birth name is not Peramal! It's Perla Maria. 'Peramal' was just a nickname. Oh, how could I have been so stupid!" Eric put his hand on his wife's hand and tried to comfort her.

"Well, that could explain everything," Mr. Torres said as he corrected the name in his notebook. Then he turned to Mari and said, "Don't be too hard on yourself, ma'am; this is all a part of the process. We just keep asking questions until we find the answers."

Eric stood up to show Xavier to the door.

"Dr. Ruiz, I will get right on it, and I will be in touch as soon as I can. You folks have a good night," Xavier said before he left.

"Thank you. Good night."

Eric closed the front door and locked it. When he turned back around, the sitting room was empty.

"Mari? *¿Mi corazón?* Where did you go?" He looked around the house and finally found his wife sitting in the dark, with tears silently rolling down her face as she sat in a rocking chair in the room that the kids used to share.

"Are you OK, *mi amor*?" Eric went to his wife and sat on the bed across from her.

"Not really. Katherine didn't know that 'Peramal' was a nickname. So that means when she tried to call the police and hospitals in New York, she did couldn't find her because she didn't have the right name."

It broke Eric's heart to see his wife suffering like that, but he couldn't say anything to make her feel better. All he could do was hold her as she cried in his arms.

Chapter 16

Peramal was working feverishly to get through the day. She wanted to be able to get home and study for a final on Saturday. She had two more semesters, and then she would finally be able to graduate. But this was a particularly long day; she recently had been assigned a business office to clean, so she had to work in the after-hours. The advantage to that situation was that she was getting paid time and a half—the additional money came in very handy.

As luck would have it, the location was close to her apartment, and she could be there in five minutes if she had to. But thankfully, that wasn't necessary; Victor was old enough now and he was trustworthy enough that she did not have to worry about Melinda.

It was a hot and humid evening in May, and the clock struck eight o'clock as she was putting the finishing touches on the large conference room. Her work was done, and everything was spotless. Peramal took pride in her work and was very meticulous. Most of the customers would request Peramal to clean their homes, so her boss had to keep juggling her schedule to make everyone happy. Peramal was one of this best employees.

Peramal had gathered her cleaning supplies and vacuum and was heading out the door when she heard her cell phone ring. She quickly looked to make sure that it wasn't Victor. She didn't recognize the number, so she let it go to voicemail. A few seconds later, it made a dinging sound, indicating that there was a message. She had recently gotten a cell phone, and she had to teach herself how to use it. But one of things that she still didn't know how to do was retrieve voicemails. She had to remember to ask Victor to help her with that when she got home.

She looked at her watch and noticed it was getting late. She couldn't wait to get home and take a shower and eat some dinner. Then her phone rang again as she was getting into the car. She thought it was the last number calling again, but this time it was Mckenna, so she answered the phone.

"Hello, my friend, how are you doing?" Peramal said.

"Hi, Peramal, I am good. How are you?"

"I am good. How are you and the babies?"

"Everyone is good. I hope I am not bothering you. Do you have a minute?"

"Sure, go ahead. I am packing my supplies, but we can talk."

"OK, this is really quick. I know you have your test on Saturday, and I know you are going to do great. Are you by chance available to babysit Georgie and Nikki on Sunday just for a couple of hours?"

"Yes, I can. What time do you want me to come?"

"Can you come by around eleven in the morning and stay until about one or two in the afternoon? I just need to go and get my nails done at the mall. James is at a conference in Tampa."

"Sure, no problem. I can be there. See you Sunday."

Peramal had babysat the twins on numerous occasions. Oftentimes she would bring Melinda and Victor with her, because Mckenna knew that Peramal had no one to watch her own kids. Although Victor didn't seem outwardly excited about it, Peramal knew that he enjoyed going to the Prescott house because he got to watch some of the premium sport channels.

Friday night came around, and she went to bed early so she could rest for her exams the next morning. But sleep wouldn't come. She was so nervous that she could feel her stomach was tied up in knots. When she finally fell asleep, the dreams started coming. It had been a long time since she had had these vivid, foretelling type of dreams, which usually happened when she was under a lot of stress. She saw Ms. Mari, and it was the same dream every time. Ms. Mari was sitting in a boat, and the boat was floating away. Peramal had no idea if Ms. Mari was alive or dead because she suppressed those feelings. Part of her did not want to know. Then other dreams, different bits and pieces about her life in Puerto Rico, started flashing before her eyes. She saw herself as a little girl, sitting with her father, but then that changed; she found herself standing before his coffin at his funeral, staring at his face. As she reached out to touch her father's face, he would disappear, and instead it would be Julio there, grabbing her arm with a painful grip as he dragged her inside the coffin and then slammed the lid shut. She started to scream, trying to push the lid open. With a final push, she broke through and found herself looking at the sun and blue skies reflected in Edward's eyes. A feeling of happiness overcame her as she reached out to touch his face. At last, the sound of the alarm clock interrupted her dreams. *Beep! Beep! Beep!*

Peramal jumped out of bed. She was disoriented after being woken up while she was in the middle of that dream. For a second she almost forgot that it was Saturday and that she had to get to school to take her exam. She ran around getting dressed, and then she quickly washed her face and brushed her teeth. It was eight o'clock, and she needed to be at the campus by nine sharp. She couldn't believe that she had overslept. Most mornings, she was up by five; she liked to spend time praying. But of all mornings, it had to be this one that she woke up three hours later than usual.

"Good morning, Mama," Victor said as he handed her a to-go cup filled with coffee after she walked into the kitchen. "Thought you might need this. Just the way you like it, black with two sugars."

"Oh, *mijo*! Thank you so much! You're a lifesaver!" Peramal kissed her son on the forehead as he smiled proudly.

"*Buenos días, Mamá*," Melinda spoke from behind her as she walked into the kitchen, wiping the sleep from her eyes.

"*Buenos días, mi niña*," her mother responded as she reached down to give Melinda a hug.

"OK, I need to go. Are you good, Victor? Can you get Melinda some breakfast? I'm sorry that I overslept."

"That's OK, I got it this. Now, you go! Good luck on your test!" Victor assured his mother.

"Thank you, *mi amor*. Melinda, please listen to your brother. OK?"

"*Sí, Mamá*," Melinda replied sleepily.

Peramal gathered her books, purse, and coffee and then quickly kissed her kids and left the apartment. Since it was a weekend morning, it only took ten minutes for her to get to the campus. She had time for herself to sit on the bench outside, next to a beautiful garden. The scent of the flowers filled the air, and she took a few breaths, trying to calm herself down. *Please, God, help me pass my final,* she prayed silently. Her thoughts were interrupted by her cell phone ringing. She had to dig through her purse before she finally found it. It was the same strange number from the other day. At first she hesitated, but then had decided to answer it when she was interrupted by her teacher, Mr. Young, walking by. He stopped to talk to her, and the call went to voicemail again.

"Good morning, Peramal. How are you doing?"

"Good morning, Mr. Young. I'm OK, just little nervous about the test."

"Oh, don't you worry. You are one of my top students in the class. I think you will do great."

"Thank you," Peramal replied, feeling a little embarrassed.

She always had the feeling that Mr. Young liked her more than was normal for a student-teacher relationship. On a few occasions, he had hinted that they could go out. But she always managed to let him down easily. Any type of student-and-teacher relationship outside the classroom was prohibited, and she had to remind him that there are boundaries. He was nice-looking, but he was probably a good fifteen years older than her. However, that wasn't the issue. She really wasn't looking for a relationship, and she wasn't sure if she ever would again after the abuse that she had endured from Julio. She considered that not all men were that way, as her thoughts went to Edward. He was the kindest and sweetest person she'd ever met besides Dr. Ruiz. But Edward was married, and he lived hundreds of miles away. For now, her focus was her kids and getting a new career started.

Mr. Young smiled and continued on his way to class as he said, "See you in class."

Peramal nodded and smiled.

As she was about to gather her things, she heard her friend's voice from behind her.

"Mr. Young and Peramal sitting in a tree, k-i-s-s-i-n-g!" Rosa sang, teasing her friend.

Peramal blushed.

"Rosa! Stop it! You know that I am not interested."

"I know you are not, but I hate to break it to you, he's in *loooove* with you!" Rosa said, laughing, as she put her arm around her friend.

"Would you stop that, please! Everyone can hear you!" Peramal continued to turn bright red.

"Well, you better be careful he doesn't go for it and ask you out. As of today, you can't use that excuse about the teacher-student thing. The class will be over."

Peramal was too caught up between her responsibilities with her job, school, and the kids that she had never considered that. It also dawned on her that if and when the time came that she was ready for a relationship, she couldn't do anything about it, because she was still married to Julio. She pushed all of these things out of her mind and went into the classroom to take the test.

The test was hard, but she felt very prepared. She took her time to go through every answer twice. When she finally looked up, she didn't realize that she was one of three people that were still taking the test. The timer went off, and the test was over. The other two students quickly got up and turned in their tests before Peramal could. She was the last one, and she wanted to leave the class before Mr. Young would have the chance to talk to her. But it was too late.

"Peramal?"

"Yes, Mr. Young?" Peramal held her breath, not knowing what he was going to say.

"You forgot to fill in your name on the test."

"Oh, I'm so sorry." Peramal was relieved as she walked back to his desk to take the test from his hand. She filled in the information and returned it to his desk.

"This was a great class. Have a nice summer," she mumbled as she turned away and headed for the door, but again she was stopped in her tracks with his question.

"If you have some time, would you like to have some coffee? School is over now."

For a moment Peramal didn't know how to respond, and thought about making an excuse. But then she realized that she just needed to be honest.

"Mr. Young. I am very flattered, but things are really complicated for me right now. There is so much that you don't know about me."

"Well, I would like to get to know you better."

"I am not so sure you do. You see, I'm married, and I have two kids, a fourteen-year-old son and a seven-year-old daughter."

Mr. Young appeared taken aback. "Well now, that does put a damper on things, doesn't it?"

"Sorry about that. Thank you. Bye!" Peramal quickly mumbled as she ran out of the classroom.

That evening Peramal wanted to celebrate finishing her finals. She felt good about them and was hopeful that she had done well.

"*Mis amores*, how about we go out to dinner? Where would you like to go?"

"I want a cheeseburger, please, with lots of fries and a chocolate milkshake!" Melinda spoke up first, and Victor agreed.

A couple of hours later, they got back from dinner and settled down in front of the TV. Peramal had finally remembered to ask her son to help her retrieve her voicemails.

Peramal

She started listening to the messages. Luckily, there were only two new messages. She was glad that she didn't have more, considering that she hadn't checked in a week or so.

The first message was from the last Wednesday evening, at eight o'clock. It was Ms. Mari's voice; she sounded desperate.

"Hello, this message is for Peramal. My name is Mari. I really need to reach her. Please call me back. Anyone!"

Peramal turned ghost-white, and she dropped the phone on the floor, startling her kids.

"Mama? Are you OK? You don't look so good." Victor came to her side first and picked up the phone.

"I'm fine. I think?" Peramal was in a state of shock. "Could it be? I mean, is it possible?"

Melinda started to get worried as she hugged her mother. "Mama? Mama? What's wrong?"

"Nothing's wrong. Everything is right. It's a miracle. She's alive." Peramal was in shock. She tried to wrap her head around the newfound information.

Victor played back the messages, and when he heard Abuelita's voice, he too broke down in tears.

"Who's alive? Why is everybody crying!" Melinda exclaimed as she too started to cry, even though she didn't know why.

"*Mija*! Abuelita is alive! Thank God! She's alive!" Peramal grabbed both of her children into her arms as the three of them started to laugh and cry at the same time.

"Wait! I have to call her back!" Peramal stood up and grabbed her cell phone.

She clicked on the missed call. The line rang about five times before she heard a woman's voice answer the phone.

"Ms. Mari? It's Peramal."

"Peramal? Is it really you?" Mari screamed at the other end of the line. "I have waited so long to hear your voice. Are you OK? Are the kids OK?"

"Yes, yes! We are good. I am so sorry that I didn't get to your messages until now."

"That's OK, *mija*. I am just so happy to hear your voice."

"We have so much catching up to do. Are you back in Puerto Rico?"

"Yes, we are. You are in Florida, right?"

"Yes. How did you know where to find me?"

"It's a long story."

They talked for the next couple of hours. Peramal told her bits and pieces about the last couple of years, leaving out some things about being homeless. She thought it would be too much for Ms. Mari handle right now.

In turn, Mari filled Peramal in on what had happened to Julio. In actuality, Peramal was not surprised and had always known that this would eventually happen. She did try and warn Julio many times. They went on further to discuss plans for Peramal and the kids to fly back to Puerto Rico. Since it was summertime, it would be the perfect time. Mari had offered that she and Eric would come to Florida if it would be easier, but Peramal did not want to put the stress of travel on Mari. Besides, Peramal really wanted to go back. She needed to resolve the issues with Julio and perhaps start the divorce proceedings. Now that Julio was in jail, it probably would make it easier on her. Part of her was hoping that Julio had changed and they could make things work, but she knew that was wishful thinking.

"*Mija*, give me your address so we can send you the tickets."

"Ms. Mari, you don't have to buy the tickets. I will save up to buy them."

"That's nonsense. You let us buy them now, and you could pay us back, *sí?*"

Even though Mari suggested Peramal paying her back, Peramal knew that Mari would never follow through and take the money. But Peramal had no choice but to give in. She really wanted to go back home to Puerto Rico.

"OK. I need to talk to my boss about taking the time off. He is pretty flexible; I am sure it won't be a problem."

"Don't you worry; even if it is a problem, Eric and I will always help take care of you! Just come back—we really miss you and our grandchildren!"

The sound of that put a big smile on Peramal's face.

"OK, *mija*. We will see you in a couple of weeks. I can't wait!"

"Me either! Take care and say 'hello' to Dr. Ruiz. Love you!"

It was almost midnight by the time Peramal hung up her cell phone. She got up from the couch, looking for her kids. She found them fast asleep in their beds.

She washed up and went to bed. It took only five minutes before she fell asleep and was having wonderful dreams about being back in Puerto Rico and reunited with Ms. Mari and Dr. Ruiz. But there was a darker side to her dream: she found Julio lurking in the shadows waiting, watching, and ready to pounce.

Chapter 17

"Abuelita! Abuelo!" Melinda screamed with excitement when she spotted her adoptive grandparents waiting in the international airport terminal in San Juan. She ran so fast that Peramal and Victor couldn't keep up with her. They trailed behind her carrying the luggage.

"Melinda! Oh, sweet girl! I have missed you!" Ms. Mari exclaimed as she jumped up from her seat to reach out and give Melinda hug. "You have grown so much!"

"It's Abuelo's turn!" Eric stood up and went over to join in their hug.

Ms. Mari then narrowed her eyes, scanning the large crowd of people walking in different directions, trying to find Peramal and Victor. Then she saw Victor—he looked so much like his father at that age, but she knew the similarity would end there.

Finally, she saw Peramal. If it weren't for Victor walking next to her, she would have never recognized her. She couldn't believe how much she had changed. Gone was the scared, helpless young woman; now Peramal looked self-assured and confident, and not to mention more beautiful than ever.

"*¡Mija!* Is that you? I don't believe it! I almost didn't recognize you!" Mari walked to meet them halfway. "Look at you! You are so beautiful!"

Peramal hugged Mari so tight that her arms ached, but she didn't care. She was so happy. "You are too kind!"

"And Victor! You're so tall! Come here, *mijo*! Give your old abuelita a hug!"

"Hi, Abuelita! You are not old; you look awesome!" Victor towered over his adoptive grandmother, so he had to bend down to put his arms around her.

Peramal went over to give Dr. Ruiz a hug and kiss on his tear-stained cheek.

"Peramal, it is so good to see you again. We didn't think we ever would," Eric said in a gruff voice.

"It is so good to see you too, Dr. Ruiz," Peramal replied as she wiped the tears from her face.

"OK! Time to go home! I made your favorite, *arroz con pollo*!" Mari spoke as she grabbed Melinda's and Peramal's hands while Eric and Victor got the luggage.

In the car, Peramal and Ms. Mari sat in the backseat, with Melinda sitting in between them, while Victor sat up front with Dr. Ruiz.

Peramal stared out the window. Everything looked the same; it was like the city had frozen in time and was exactly as she had remembered it. She had mixed emotions. Part of her was happy, but she was also afraid because all of the bad memories that came rushing back. Fear and anxiety welled up inside her, and she started to hyperventilate. She wasn't sure if she could get herself to go in the house where she had lived with Julio.

Ms. Mari noticed her distress, and she reached to grab her hand.

"Peramal? Are you OK?"

"Yes. I'm fine." Peramal tried to smile, but she wasn't fooling anyone, especially Ms. Mari.

"We're home!" Eric announced as he pulled up in front of the house. There were beautiful, green hedges surrounded by lots of different flowers and giant trees; the hedges created an archway along the length of the driveway. The house was a single story, with a Spanish-style tiled roof, and it spread out over at least an acre. Peramal was too caught up in a moment of panic and anxiety to notice where they were going.

"But where are we? Whose house is this? I thought we were going to your house, Ms. Mari?" Peramal was confused, but relieved at the same time.

"No, *mija*. We sold that house, and we bought this one." Ms. Mari smiled and gave Peramal a knowing look. "We thought it might be better for you to visit us here."

"You did not have to that on my account. This house looks really expensive!"

"Don't you worry about that, Peramal. I made some really good investments, and Ms. Mari and I are perfectly fine!" Eric reassured her. "Now, who wants to see the house?"

"I do!" Melinda exclaimed as she climbed over Peramal to get out of the car and ran up the steps to the front door, ahead of everyone.

After they got settled in and ate dinner, Peramal sat on the veranda with Ms. Mari and Eric as they enjoyed the evening breeze and watched the sun set. Melinda and Victor were out of earshot, watching TV and playing video games.

Out of the blue, Peramal announced, "I want to go and see Julio." The older couple were taken by surprise, but they also understood why.

"*Mija*, I understand why you want to go but you also have to know something: he has a lot of anger and hostility toward you. I am not sure what purpose it will serve."

"I need the closure, and I also wanted to tell him face-to-face that I am filing for a divorce. I am no longer that scared teenage girl that he can push or punch around."

"But you don't need to see him in person. You can work through a lawyer. Isn't that right, *mi corazón*?" Ms. Mari turned to her husband, looking for confirmation.

"That's true, Peramal. I can call my lawyer who handled my divorce," Eric offered. "If I am not mistaken, this might be a special circumstance, since he is in prison for a felony. They probably could expedite the process, and he would be unable to contest it."

Eric got up and walked into the house to call his lawyer on behalf of Peramal.

"Ms. Mari?" Peramal got up from her seat to sit next to her. "I'm sorry if this was my fault. I don't know if I did anything wrong to make him this way."

"*¡Mija!* You have nothing to apologize for! This is all on him." Ms. Mari went on to explain, "Hi mother, God rest her soul, tried to get him psychological help. But he would always manipulate his way out of anything, and he never got the help that he needed."

"I know. I just wish I could make it work with him, at least for the sake of his children."

"If he is too stubborn to recognize that he needs help, nothing will ever help him. I know it is not my place, but I don't think you should take the children with you. At least not the first time. You should see him on your own, and then if all goes well, take the kids with you. Right?"

"Yes. You're right." Peramal gave in on that point.

"Of course! I'm always right!" Ms. Mari declared, bringing a smile to Peramal's face.

Eric finished his phone call and came back to the veranda.

"Peramal, I got you an appointment tomorrow at nine. I can take you there."

"You don't have. I don't want to disturb you so early."

"Nonsense! I would be happy to. I am usually up at dawn, and I have an appointment in downtown too, around the same time. So it works out perfectly."

"Thank you…for everything." Peramal walked over to Dr. Ruiz and gave him a hug.

"*De nada,*" he replied as he hugged her back.

"Now, I think I need to get some sleep. I better get the kids to bed too."

"No, it's too early. Let them play a while. We'll take care of them and see that they get to bed," Ms. Mari offered. "It's their vacation; let them enjoy themselves. Besides, that way we can spend more time with them."

"OK, OK, you twisted my arm. *Buenas noches.*" Peramal smiled and bid the older couple goodnight, and then she went to bed.

The next morning, Peramal met with the lawyer, and as Eric had said, everything would be pretty straightforward. Before she started the process, she wanted to see Julio one more time. She wasn't sure why—maybe she was looking for a miracle, that Julio would become a nicer person and they would live happily ever after. If only she would be so lucky.

Her lawyer had arranged a visit at the prison on Friday, which was in two days. To Peramal, those were the longest two days of her life. She just wanted to get it over with. It turned out that Julio had tried to stab another inmate and he was spending time in solitary confinement, so she had to wait for that to be over before she could visit.

Friday finally came around. Peramal woke up at five in the morning to pray. She asked for forgiveness if she had done anything wrong, and then she asked that God help her to say the right things to Julio. She didn't know what to expect. From what Ms. Mari had told her, he was extremely vulgar and violent; Ms. Mari was afraid for Peramal. For a moment she felt like the scared and weak person whom Julio had easily intimidated. It took all her energy to fight those feelings. She was not that person anymore; that person had died a long time ago. Julio would never again get the best of her.

"Hey, Collazo, wake up! Time to go." The prison guard banged on the metal door of the jail cell. "You know what to do. Get on your stomach and put your hands behind your back."

Julio complied. He didn't want to risk getting put back in solitary again.

Two guards walked into the cell. One had the handcuffs, and the other stood by with his hand on his gun holster. They placed the handcuffs on Julio's wrists, and then they stood him up. He was walking slowly, so they had to push him along several times.

He then noticed that he wasn't being taken to his cell.

"Where are you taking me?" Julio demanded.

"You have a visitor. It's your wife."

"Peramal? She's finally here! I knew she would come!" His whole demeanor changed, and he became a different person—very arrogant and cocky.

They led him to a room where there was a thick, glass partition.

Julio stood his ground and started to argue with the guards. "Hey! Don't I get conjugal visits? I demand to be alone with my wife!"

"Sorry, buddy. Those types of visits are not allowed here."

"But she's my wife! I know my rights!"

"Take up with the judge! Now move it!"

Julio got so agitated that the guards pushed him to the ground to get him to calm down.

One of the guards warned him, "You better listen to me! You have a choice here: either you calm down, and we take you to see your wife; or you go back in solitary. Which is it going to be?"

"OK, OK!" Julio agreed as they picked up him to get him on his feet.

They finally made it to the visitation room, and he saw her sitting at the other side of the thick, glass window. He had forgotten how beautiful she was. Julio sat down on the cold steel chair as he kept staring at her, like he was in a trance. He was going through a battle of wills inside of himself. He wanted so desperately to apologize to his wife and ask for her forgiveness. He wanted to tell her that he truly did love her and was sick to his stomach every time he thought about the abuse he had inflicted on her. But the dark side of him won, and it showed no mercy.

Peramal reached over to grab the receiver at the same time as Julio.

"Hello, Julio. Are you OK?"

"Why do you care, bitch? It's your fault that I am in here; I hope you're happy!"

Peramal was taken aback by his accusation and name calling. Once again she found herself feeling intimidated and scared of him.

"Why are you saying that? You know it is not true! I tried to warn you so many times, but you never listened to me!"

"That bullshit that you could see the future—a lot of good it did you. You married me, remember? Not so psychic after all, are you?"

"Did you ever love me? Did you?" She was on the verge of tears, and she was struggling not show him how much he was getting to her.

Peramal

Julio wanted to say, *Yes! Yes! Yes! And I still do! Please don't leave me!*

But instead, he said, "I guess. Maybe. If you count that I loved to fuck you, then I guess I did."

"Why do you have to be so cruel! What about the kids? Do you even care about them?"

"Nope. They are probably not even mine. I knew you were a cheating whore. But that's OK, I will still keep you around when I get out. You are good at spreading your legs and that's good enough for me—a real nice, tight pussy."

Peramal was mortified and felt herself turn a dark shade of red. She couldn't handle it anymore. She had to go, but not before she said her piece.

"You are never going to change. You need help, and I hope that you get it someday. Part of me will always care about you because you are the father of my children. But I am moving on with my life. I thought maybe I could give it a chance, but it does not look like it is possible. Until you recognize that you need help, you will never get better. I will be filing for a divorce and…"

Julio interrupted Peramal before she finished her sentence.

"You can't fuckin' divorce me! I will not sign any papers. You got that, bitch?"

"Hate to break it to you, you have no choice. The law is on my side. You are a convicted felon; I have every right." It felt good to put him in his place. She couldn't believe that she had finally done it.

Peramal hung up the receiver and stood up, pushing her chair back while never taking her eyes off of Julio. He sat there with a stunned look on his face. She gave him one last look and walked away with her head held high. Before she made to the exit door, she heard a loud bang come from behind her. She turned to find Julio punching the glass window. The blow was so hard that she could see the window starting to crack.

He looked so angry as he was screaming for her to come back, and then he proceeded to call her every name in the book.

"Peramal! Come back here! Fuckin' bitch! You can't walk away from me! I am your husband!"

Peramal kept going and never looked back at him.

She made her way out of the prison office and walked toward her car. To her left she noticed that there was a prison bus parked, and the guards were unloading a group of inmates. She happened to notice one of the prisoner's faces. It looked familiar. She couldn't believe who she was seeing—it was Cousin Alberto. He happened to glance up and found her staring at him. Peramal just smiled and waved and got into her car. Shock didn't even begin to describe the look on his face as he saw her drive away.

Chapter 18

May came around again, and Peramal was finally going to graduate from the technical school. Plus, she had just found out that she had been accepted into the police-academy training program that was going to start in June. Her dreams were coming true, one by one. The plan was that she would train at the police academy, and then she could work in the crime-scene-investigating unit. She was so excited that every now and then, she would pinch herself to make sure that she wasn't dreaming. Her divorce was finalized in less than six months, and she was a free woman, though she was definitely not interested in jumping into a relationship. All she wanted to do was work, do a good job, and take care of her family.

It was the morning of the last day that she would be working for the cleaning service. She went into her kitchen and found Ms. Mari sitting there drinking her coffee. Ms. Mari and Eric had arrived the night before from Puerto Rico. They had wanted to come and spend the rest of the year there, to help Peramal with the kids while she was attending the academy and to be there for her graduation. Eric had a condo in Safety Harbor that he had been renting out. The current occupants were snowbirds who would soon be heading back up to Connecticut for awhile; Dr. Ruiz and Mari had to wait a week before it was available. In the meantime they would stay with Peramal. They had offered to stay at a hotel, but Peramal wouldn't take "no" for an answer to her invitation.

"*Buenos días*, Ms. Mari. Did you guys sleep well?" Peramal went over to pour herself a cup of coffee.

"*Buenos días*, *mija*. Yes, we are fine. We are happy to be here with you and the kids."

"Good, I'm glad to hear that. I have to leave in a few minutes. I should be home by two thirty."

"Do you have to go to work? But it's a Saturday."

"I know. I usually don't work on Saturdays, but my boss asked me to do this house for a new client, and he will pay me extra. It also worked out because you're here to watch the kids."

"Where do you have to go?"

"Clearwater Beach. My boss was contacted by the realtor, and they wanted to have the house spotless before the buyer showed up. I think it's a pretty big house, so it will take me about four hours, or maybe less because there is no one living there yet."

"Oh, by the way, Eric wants to take you and kids out tonight for dinner. So think about where you want to go."

"Ms. Mari, you guys don't have to do that. I can pick up some groceries on my way home, and I can cook."

"We won't hear of it. You need time to relax, and now you can, with us here. Eric can be very stubborn, so don't even try to argue with him. ¿Sí?"

Peramal

Peramal smiled and went over to give Ms. Mari a hug. Then she got ready for work and told Mari that if she needed anything for herself or the kids, to give Peramal a call.

The drive to the house took about twenty minutes. It was the start of summer and the beaches were busy, so it took a little extra time. Thankfully, there was no there waiting on her.

She gathered her cleaning supplies and vacuum and walked to a side door, as Jack had instructed her. There was a lock box with the key. Then, she called the office to get the number.

The house was beautiful, and right on the water. The inside of the house was even more breathtaking than the outside: hardwood floors and some areas with shiny marble. If she didn't know any better, she'd think it looked like the house she had seen in her dreams. *Yeah, like that would ever come true,* she thought to herself. But she didn't care, money wasn't everything. She was on her way to getting a good job, and that was all that mattered.

She worked diligently from room to room. Every so often she would call the apartment to make sure that Melinda and Victor were not giving Ms. Mari and Dr. Ruiz a hard time.

Three and half hours later, Peramal was done. She just finished mopping the wood floors upstairs when she was startled by male voices coming from downstairs. There was a moment of panic, because she had been told no one would be coming to the house that day. She ran to the window to look outside: there were two cars. Relief set in when she noticed that one of the cars had a sign on the door identifying it as belonging to a real-estate agent.

She gathered her things and quickly went down the stairs and into the kitchen, where the side door that she'd come into earlier in the day was located. The two men made their way to the patio through a sliding-glass door from the family room. One of the men was holding the hand of a young child, probably no more than five years of age.

She realized that was her chance to get out unseen. She had quickly collected her cleaning products and vacuum and had turned to walk out the door when she was stopped by the sound of a small voice greeting her.

"Hi. What are you doing?" the little boy asked. Peramal turned back around and responded with a "hello."

"My name is Joseph; what's your name?" he said as he climbed up a stool that was next to the counter.

"Hi, Joseph, my name is Peramal. I was cleaning the house. But now I have to go."

"Hi, Pimar. This is my new house, and you're pretty. You wanna see the pool? It's really big." He stretched out his little arms trying to show her how big it was. "But my daddy said that I am not allowed near it until I learn to swim. He is going to put a fence around it. Do you have pool?"

"Well, your house is beautiful, and thank you for the compliment. I'm late, and I really must go." Peramal was desperate to get out, but this adorable little boy was asking a lot of questions. He had light-blond hair and the bluest eyes she had ever seen—except maybe for Edward's eyes. She hadn't thought about Edward for months now, and all of sudden she couldn't stop thinking about him. *Where is he, and what is he doing now?* she wondered.

"It was nice meeting you, Joseph. Now, why don't you go back out there? I am sure your father is looking for you."

"OK! Bye!" The little boy scrambled off the stool and ran back to the patio.

Once more, she picked up her supplies and vacuum, and this time she made it out the door.

As she was getting into her car, she took one last look at the outside of the house. There was something familiar about it, but she couldn't quite put her finger on it.

For a second, she thought about going back inside to meet the new owner. But, she changed her mind when her cell phone rang. It was her daughter, asking her when she was coming home because she was hungry.

Chapter 19

The next couple of weeks went by quickly, and soon the day had come for her to start her training at the academy. She was so nervous, it felt like her stomach was tied in knots. It was a rough first week until she was able to get with the program. It took both physical and mental endurance, but she was up to the challenge. Every night when she got home, she barely managed to eat a bite because she was too tired. She usually went straight to bed. Peramal was so thankful for Ms. Mari and Dr. Ruiz. They had the kids move in with them so that she could focus all her energy on completing the training. On the weekends, she would spend as much time as she could with them.

It was the final six weeks of the program; the training was coming to an end. Since that year's class was larger than usual, the police-academy management had to break it up into two groups for the specialized training in the crime-scene-investigation portion. They were bringing in a consultant to assist with the course. There was a sign-up sheet for those who volunteered to work with the consultant. It didn't take long before all but one spot was taken. The rumor was that the consultant was a hot-shot, decorated police officer from New York—so he was in high demand. She stood staring at the list pinned to the bulletin board. Although Peramal had made up her mind to stay where she was, she had a nagging feeling that she should sign up. As she was about to reach up and put her name, one of the other rookies got their first and took the spot. *Oh well,* she thought to herself. *I guess it was not meant to be.* She was perfectly fine with her current instructor, and besides, she wanted to keep her schedule with the morning class because the other was in the afternoon.

The weeks melted away, and Peramal was finally graduating from the police academy. She couldn't believe that she had finally done it. Ms. Mari and Dr. Ruiz wanted to have a party to celebrate, but Peramal refused. She just wanted to go out for a nice dinner with the people that she loved. Mckenna and her family wouldn't be able to make it; they were staying in Australia for several months. James's father had passed, and he had to be there for his mother to get the estate and ranch business in order. Mckenna promised Peramal that they would get together to celebrate when she was back in town.

"A toast to Peramal! Congratulations!" Dr. Ruiz had raised his glass of wine in honor of her graduation. It was a December evening, and it was still quite warm, although they were expecting a cold front within the next two weeks. They were sitting outside at Peramal's favorite restaurant on the beach.

"Thank you, everyone! I will also raise my glass to you all, my wonderful family, for putting up with me when I was grouchy these last few months," Peramal replied with her own toast.

"What, you? Grouchy? Never!" Ms. Mari teased. "You were sweet as pie!"

"I'm sorry, I didn't mean to be." she apologized as she sat back down and took a sip from her wineglass.

"I'm only teasing you, *mija*. I am very proud of you. You have come a long way."

"I know. Thank you. I just wish…oh, never mind."

"Wish what? Tell me."

"I wish that I could find my mother…" Ms. Mari stopped smiling and visibly flinched. Then Peramal realized that she had hurt her feelings. "I'm so sorry, I didn't mean for that to hurt your feelings."

"That's OK, *mija*. You don't have to explain."

"Yes, I do! You are the greatest mother that I could ever ask for. I don't know what I did to deserve you. I just want to have closure on that part of my life so I can move forward. Does that make sense?"

"Of course it does." Ms. Mari looked a little relieved and started smiling again. Peramal reached over and gave her a hug. "OK, who wants dessert? How about a huge piece of chocolate cake and ice cream!"

"Yeah! Ice cream and cake!" Melinda started jumping for joy in her chair.

Just as Peramal was about to get the attention of the server, she noticed a young boy coming toward her, gesturing in her direction to the man following him. She saw his blond head make its way between the tables.

"See, Daddy! That's her! The lady that was at our house a long time ago! That's Pimar!" Joseph shouted, bringing attention of the other diners to their table.

Peramal finally realized that the boy was Joseph.

"Hi, Joseph! It is so nice to see you again!" She was so focused on the little boy that she didn't realize the man with him was staring at her in disbelief.

"Hi, Pimar! This is my daddy!"

She finally looked up to greet his father, only to find that his father was Edward.

Chapter 20

Peramal could feel the warm sand trickle down her back as she got up from the beach and turned toward the sound coming from behind her. The sun was hot and it was humid, but it was still another beautiful September day in Clearwater Beach. She shielded her eyes from the sun, forgetting that her sunglasses were on top of her head. The voice was getting louder and louder, and she could barely make out the person coming toward her.

"No! No! No! This can't be!" She turned back around, ignoring the voice behind her and sat back down on the beach and closed her eyes and started praying. "Oh God! Please let this be real! This is not a dream! This is not a dream!"

That was how Edward found her when he got to her side. He knelt down in front of her, putting his hands on either side of her face.

"Darling, what's wrong? Open your eyes. Are you OK?" Edward said, with concern in his voice.

Peramal opened her eyes slowly and found Edward's beautiful blues staring back at her.

"Edward, are you...are you *real*?"

"Yes, sweetheart, I'm real. Can't you feel me touching your face?" Edward was getting more worried. "I think you got too much sun; let's go in."

"In where?" she hesitated.

"Our house. You know, where you have been living since we got married a year ago?" He gave her a quizzical look.

"Our house?" she asked and then suddenly it was like a light went off! "Oh! Oh! Thank you, God! This is not a dream!" Peramal jumped up and hugged her husband so tight that it was hard for him to breathe, but he didn't mind. Then she noticed the rings on her left hand, which were brightly shimmering in the sun. The diamond solitaire was huge, at least three carats, and it was complemented by an equally beautiful matching wedding band.

"You had me scared for a minute. What happened?"

"Well, let me try to explain this so you won't think that I am crazy. Remember that night that we met in the park?"

"Yeah, I remember. How could I forget? I think that I fell in love with you that night." Then he bent down and gave her a kiss. "OK. So, go on—that night at the park..." he prompted.

"I never told you this, but I was having a dream about a situation like this, being on a beach with a beautiful house and my husband was calling me," she explained. "I think the last time I had that dream, it was the night in New York. So when it happened now, I was afraid I was dreaming again and none of this was real, and...." Her voice trailed off as she looked for a sign that Edward didn't think she was crazy. "Am I making any sense?"

"Nope. But that's OK, because I wouldn't have it any other way! We gotta go and pack and drop off the kids at their grandparents!" Edward said as he started walking toward the house, urging Peramal to go with him.

"Where are we going?"

"To the airport, remember? We have a flight to catch!"

In that moment, it came back to her. Edward had finally located her mother, who was living in Phoenix. That was where they were going.

After they had reconnected at the restaurant the night of her celebration dinner, everything had fallen into place. If she had only followed her instincts, she would have gone back into the house where she had met Joseph; if so, she would have seen Edward. But it didn't matter; fate had brought them back together, and it was all thanks to a persistent little boy.

Edward filled her in on his life over the last few of years. After he found his wife cheating on him with an old boyfriend, Edward had divorced her and taken custody of his son. Cecelia didn't care to have custody; she wanted to be single and free.

He had continued to play the lottery, and eventually Edward won millions of dollars, just as Peramal had predicted. He left the New York Police Department and moved down to Florida with Joseph to be closer to his mother, Joseph's grandmother. Edward had been hoping that he would run into Peramal since he knew that she had wanted to go there, at some point, to look for her mother.

Since Edward was not exactly ready to retire, he started a security-consulting firm and taught at the police academy.

Then came another realization: Peramal figured out that he was the hot-shot police officer from New York, and if she had signed up for that course, they would have met months earlier. Again, it didn't matter because it was better late than never.

Peramal went to work at the police department in the crime-scene-investigation unit. Her gift came in handy to help guide the decisions that she made every day. She planned to work there to get as much experience as she could under her belt, because eventually she wanted to work with Edward in his consulting company.

After a relatively short courtship, Edward asked Dr. Ruiz for Peramal's hand in marriage, and Dr. Ruiz agreed. But it wasn't easy; it took a lot for Edward to gain Dr. Ruiz's trust. Peramal was like a daughter to him, and he wanted to make sure that she wouldn't be hurt as she had been in the past. Now, here they were, happily married.

They had had a small wedding ceremony, and Peramal wore the white dress that she had always dreamed about. She had asked Dr. Ruiz to give her away, and he was very honored. Meanwhile, Ms. Mari was the very emotional mother-of-the-bride. Melinda was her maid of honor, and Victor, the best man. Joseph was the ring bearer, along with the Prescott twins as the flower girls. It was a beautiful and magical day that no one was going to forget; they would always cherish it.

However, there was one missing piece that Peramal needed to find, and that was her mother. The advent of social media made it easier for Edward to track her down. She was remarried and living in Arizona.

Now, Edward and Peramal were sitting at the Tampa International Airport, waiting for their flight to Phoenix. A particular brand of new smartphone had just come out, and Edward had bought one. He was like a kid in a toy store, excited about pushing buttons and making things light up. He so distracted playing that he didn't notice that Peramal was looking pale—she was breathing hard and on the verge of hyperventilating. She was overthinking about every scenario of what could happen if and when she finally confronted her mother. Did she really want to know the truth? Maybe it would be too much for her to bear? She tried to remind herself that she was not that scared little girl anymore. She finally had everything she wanted and more—a wonderful, loving husband; a beautiful family; and a great job.

"Sweetheart, check this out." Edward looked over at his wife with a smile on his face. But his smile quickly faded when he noticed she was in distress.

"Hey, it's OK. Take a deep breath. I know you are nervous about going. If you don't want to go, we can go home; just say the word." He reached over to rub her back as he tried to comfort her. "It's been over twenty years; another few days won't make a difference."

She was finally able to speak, but she still sounded out of breath.

"No, I want to go. I have to do this. I will be all right." She leaned over onto his shoulder. "Can you do something for me?

"Of course, anything!"

"Hold me," she whispered softly.

"Come here," he said as he folded her into his arms over the armrest of the airport chair and held her.

After a few minutes, he asked, "Are you doing all right, my love?"

She smiled up at him. "Yes, much better, thank you."

He bent down and kissed her forehead. "I'm glad."

"You know, almost all my life people treated me badly. I was always told that I wasn't good enough or smart enough; maybe that was why everybody found it easy to leave me or turn me away."

Peramal was so lost in thought that she didn't realize that she was saying this out loud until she heard Edward vehemently disagreeing with her.

"Darling, please don't say that! You know it is not true!"

"I know that now. But back then, when I heard it all the time, especially from people who were supposed to be my family, I believed them."

"Well, I am going to make sure to remind you that you are good enough and smart enough every day for the rest of our lives together!"

Peramal sat up from her leaning position to face Edward.

"You already have, back in New York."

Edward looked confused and asked, "What do you mean?"

"That Saturday morning at the park, when I asked you why you became a police officer and then I told you that was something that I had always thought of doing."

"Oh, that's right. I remember that." He smiled softly, remembering how adorable she had looked and how much he wanted to kiss her. "I hope you know that I really meant it."

"I know you did. What you didn't realize how good you made me feel when you encouraged me and then helped me get started with completing my GED."

Their conversation was interrupted by the gate attendant speaking on the intercom.

"Flight four twenty-two to Phoenix is now ready for boarding; please line up according to group number."

Edward looked at Peramal. "Are you ready for this?"

"As ready as I will ever be," she replied as they gathered their belongings.

"That's my girl." Edward grabbed her hand and kissed it softly. Then they walked hand in hand to board the plane.

Chapter 21

The flight to Phoenix was uneventful. Peramal enjoyed all the perks of flying first class so much that part of her didn't want the flight to end, or maybe she had gotten cold feet and wanted to delay getting there.

They arrived at the resort and spa around midnight. Edward wanted his wife to be as comfortable as possible. He planned that they would enjoy the amenities at the spa the following day, Saturday. Then, on Sunday, they would drive out to the address where her mother lived.

According to the detective that Edward had worked with to track down Iris, she lived in a nice part of town. Her new husband owned a chain of carwashes, and they were doing well financially. The detective had monitored their activities and noted that her mother was usually home alone on Sunday mornings because her husband was out playing golf. Peramal agreed with Edward about going there when they knew that the new husband would not likely be home. The less people around, the less drama there would be.

"OK, I guess this is it," Peramal said as she let out a long, slow breath, relieving some of her anxiety. It was Sunday morning, and she and Edward were sitting in a rental car parked across the street and a few houses down from her mother's address. She finally worked up the nerve to get out of the car.

Edward offered to go with her.

"I can come with you if you want."

"Thank you, but I need to go alone."

"OK. You can do this. I love you," he said as he reached over to give her a quick kiss on the lips.

"I love you more. Wish me luck."

"Always." Edward smiled.

Peramal was shaking as she walked over to the house. It was a nice two-story with a perfectly manicured lawn and a white-picket fence.

She reached the door and quickly rang the bell before she lost her nerve.

It was only a few seconds, but it felt like an eternity. Then the door swung open, and there she was, Peramal's mother. Although it looked like she had had work done on her face trying to regain her youth, the twenty-five years since Peramal had last seen her had definitely taken their toll on her—this was evident in her tired eyes. She had thick makeup on and bright-red lipstick. Her platinum-blond hair, obviously colored, was perfectly coiffed, with not a hair out of place.

"Hello, mother dear. Nice to see you again after all these years." Peramal couldn't keep the sarcasm out of her voice. "Aren't you going to invite your long-lost daughter in?"

Peramal

Iris was in absolute shock and speechless. The last time she had seen Peramal was when she was eight years old, but she immediately recognized her even after all those years. Peramal had her father's eyes.

She backed up, allowing the door to open further so that Peramal could walk in.

The house was decorated with expensive, ornate furniture, and a ton of paintings hung all around. On the mantle there was picture of a happy bride and groom, and Peramal recognized that the bride was her sister, Sophia. Next to that was another picture, of young children, and she guessed that those were Sophia's children because one of the girls looked exactly like Sophia when she was younger.

"I see you have done well for yourself."

Iris didn't respond; she just stood there like a deer in headlights.

"Aren't you going to say something, Mother?"

"How...how...did you find me?"

"Well, you didn't make it easy. But I found a way. I always do."

"I don't have any money here, so you better leave before I call the police," Iris threatened. Her husband was going to be home any minute, and she did not want to have to explain Peramal to him.

"So that's what you think? I am after money? Are you kidding me!" Peramal let the anger and resentment take over her. "Well, I don't *need* your money! In fact, I have money, a lot of it! And I have an incredible husband that loves and adores me, and three beautiful children that mean the world to me, who I would never ever in a million years *abandon* like you *abandoned me!*"

"Then what do you want?" Iris's voice started to tremble with guilt or fear—Peramal couldn't tell which.

"I want the truth, and I am not leaving here until I get it!"

"I left you with your grandmother; you were taken care of…"

Peramal couldn't keep it inside anymore; she made sure her mother knew everything.

"Taken care of? Is that what you call being treated like shit, degraded, used and abused, molested, and raped when I was only eight years old, and again when I was twelve! Are you kidding me? And not to mention, I was thrown out by my dear brother, A. J. and left homeless to fend for myself!"

"What do you want to know?" Iris was getting desperate, and she really wanted Peramal to leave.

"Why did you leave me? Was it because of the money? Answer me!"

"I am not sure what you mean."

"Don't lie to me, I read the letters—were they true? Did you leave me on purpose so that Abuela could use me to make money?"

"You said you read the letters…" Her mother was afraid to answer the question.

"Yes, I did read the letters, but I want to *hear* it from you. Now answer me!"

Peramal

They stood staring at each other. Peramal was not backing down.

Iris looked down to the floor because she couldn't face her daughter when she finally answered a barely audible "yes."

"I want you to look at me when you say it."

Tears and mascara were streaming down her mother's face when she finally looked up and repeated, "Yes."

Although Peramal already knew the answer, hearing it directly from her mother felt like someone had punched her in the stomach.

"That is all I needed to hear. Have a nice life."

Peramal headed toward the front door. But then something made her stop and turn around. "Oh, by the way, Mother, you should go and get a brain scan. There might be something that will go *pop!* It might be nothing, but you should get it checked out anyway."

"Why are you saying that?" her mother said, on the verge of hysterics. "I don't believe you! You're lying!"

"Really? That's ironic, considering that you believed in my gift enough to leave me behind so you could make money off of me. You chose money over your daughter, remember? But don't worry, you'll be fine. *¡Adiós!*"

Peramal turned back around and made it out the door this time.

She saw Edward standing outside the car, leaning against it waiting for her. He stood up when he saw her coming. Peramal quickly crossed the street and finally made it to the car and into his waiting arms. He gave her a hug and held her tight for minute and then asked, "Are you OK?"

"Never better. Let's get out of here."

"You got it." Edward was surprised that his wife seemed happy and relaxed.

They quickly got into the car and took off. As they were driving by the house, she saw her mother run out to the sidewalk, yelling. "Peramal! Come back here!"

Edward was concerned and started to slow the car down. "Peramal, do I need to go back?"

"No, just keep driving."

"Why was she doing that?"

"I told her that she might need a brain scan for an aneurysm. But she shouldn't worry because she will OK."

"Oh no! Is that true?"

"Nah, I was just messing with her!" Peramal started laughing to the point of tears. "You should have seen the look on her face!"

"Oh my darling, you are bad! But I must say, she did deserve it." Her husband joined in the laughter.

And with that, Peramal was able to close the chapter on that part of her life. She could finally look forward to the future she had in store with Edward and their kids. But, the past was not too far behind.

About the Author

Mila Toterah is originally from southern California. Currently, she lives on the west coast of Florida with her husband and two children. In the novel, *Peramal*, Mila tells the real-life story of a remarkable young woman who has suffered so much in her life and how she overcame those odds. It is indeed very true that Peramal can read the future. It is also true that she uses her gift to help others but without financial gain.

Made in the USA
Middletown, DE
20 January 2018